Kate H

By

Michael J May

Contents

Introduction.		5
1.	Tiddington, Warwickshire, 21 July 2025.	6
2.	Waiting to happen.	16
3.	She Chameleon.	24
4.	Where Paranoia Roams.	36
5.	Apprentice Seductress.	44
6.	Unleashing the Stranger from a Kiss.	52
7.	A Heart Void of Remorse.	60
8.	Nervous Anticipation.	66
9.	Regrets can't Mend a Loss.	72
10.	Cirrus Clouds Above.	78
11.	The Violent Silence.	82
12.	Hold Me Like You Mean It.	90
13.	Darkness Know Not My Heart!	94
14.	The Air You Breathe.	101
15.	The Art of Solitude.	108
16.	Dancing Shadows.	116
17.	A Perfect Cast of Misfits.	127

18.	Circumstances in G Minor.	136
19.	Maternal Soliloquies.	146
20.	Metamorphosis in Pink.	167
21.	The Angel of Fondness.	172
22.	Above us, the Stars.	178
23.	Wallflower Blossom.	187
24.	Tragedy Behind a Mask.	192
25.	Absolution in the Absence of Sin.	196
26.	A Clash of Emotions.	203
27.	Merry Christmas, Mr Lawrence.	208
28.	Abigail's Nightmare.	211
29.	Actions, Consequences.	220
30.	Outro.	232
31.	Alternate Ending.	233
1.	Merry Christmas, Mr Lawrence.	234
2.	The Lights Die Down.	237

INTRODUCTION.

This book requires an introduction.
Or, to be more precise, requires an explanation.
There are two books to this story; Kate H is one of them, and Abigail is the other.

These books follow the same storyline, but from the perspective of different people. This book, Kate H, follows the story as Kate sees it. You get the same general story as in Abigail, same outcome, but from a different perspective. You get Kate's thoughts, impressions, feelings, issues.

It's a completely different way of reading the same story.

1. Tiddington, Warwickshire, 21 July 2025.

Rain. She hated rain. It clattered against the front window like hail on a tin roof. The cat lay on her stomach, fast asleep and oblivious to the noise.
She sighed deeply, almost waking the cat from her slumbers. It shifted uneasily, and resumed its nap.
It was almost four o'clock. She should do something. But what? The house was spotless; it looked like a show-home. Sean had disliked that side of her. But she couldn't help it; it had to be tidy. She'd paid a lot of money for this house, and the stuff contained within it. This alone dictated that it should be looked after.
She stared out at the rain as it ran down the window. It distorted the world outside, making it even more unattractive than usual. She wasn't an outgoing person. She liked the outdoors; walking, running, cycling. That wasn't the problem. It was the people. People weren't her thing. At all.
Her mother was constantly on her case, pushing her to go out more, meet people, maybe find a partner.
Or, at the very least, a new friend.
Or even just "A" friend.
She had friends of course. Well, work colleagues more like. However, she did socialise with them outside of work too occasionally, so considered them friends of sorts.
The bright flash of lightning made her jump, and the cat finally lost its patience with her.

It stretched, digging its nails into her out of protest, and then disappeared out to the kitchen in search of food.

Instinctively, she grabbed a pillow and covered her head. She knew the thunder would come.

She didn't like thunder. It was loud. Too loud.

Loud noises weren't her thing either. Was anything her thing? She had no idea.

She heard the muted rumble of thunder through the pillow, and closed her eyes. Memories from her childhood flooded back. She had loved thunder and lightning then, she would always run outside to stand in the rain and be part of the experience. What had happened to her since then? She had been carefree, outgoing, fun to be around, and happy.

Not that she wasn't happy right now of course, it was just a different kind of happiness she supposed.

Lightening flashed again, and she counted the seconds until she heard the rumble of thunder. If she remembered correctly, it was a kilometre for every seven seconds. Or, you know, something like that.

She also remembered her father telling her how they had to make a mad dash for the TV aerial connector whenever there was thunder and lightning about. It was just a thing people did back then.

Scared that the aerial would be hit and blow up the TV. Such simpler times.

No such worries nowadays of course, as all of her TV came via the broadband box. Not an aerial in sight.

The TV was on and was, of course, completely unaffected by the weather outside. It was currently showing an RSC production of *As You Like It*.

She loved Shakespeare. No, loved was not the right word. She was *obsessed.* It was her entire life. It paid the bills, bought her food, and brought her comfort. She had studied English Literature at Cambridge, and was currently working in her dream job at the Royal Shakespeare Company.

She was Kate Harrington, the Shakespeare Curriculum Product Manager at the Royal Shakespeare Company in Stratford-upon-Avon.

That meant she was in charge of the online learning catalogue of the RSC, which were to be used by institutions around the world.

She analysed all of Shakespeare's plays, making notes and interpretations for students to use in their understanding of Shakespeare's works. A team of ten people helped her, translating her words for foreign students around the globe. Her words.

People were studying her interpretations of Shakespeare's works. Not that it impressed her parents; they still hounded her to get a "proper job". Had she not proven herself? She owned her own house. Outright. Ok, so maybe that wasn't such an achievement: she had inherited £500k from her Grandmother, and had used it to buy this bungalow. Her grandmother had left money in her will to both her and her brother James.

To their parent's great relief, they had both spent the money wisely. She had used her share to buy this house near her hero's birthplace, and James had used his to buy a home on the coast near Seattle in the USA. Perhaps not quite what her parents had expected, but it had been his dream.

He was the technically brainy child. He worked as an Engineer for General Dynamics on the nearby Naval Base. She, on the other hand, had been the dreamy one. The reader. The artist. The quiet child. The complete opposite to her brother.

He had been her best friend growing up. Still was her best friend to be honest. Not difficult, given that she didn't have real friends to speak of. Fortunately, they were still close, and she knew she could depend on him if needed.

She spoke to him on WhatsApp a few times a week, and she flew over once a year for her holiday.

She still rode the bike he had built for her to work every day. Rain or shine. It was only an eight-minute ride from her house to the RSC.

Sometimes she walked, depending on what she wore, and her mood.

Her mood. Ugh. If only it wasn't so dark sometimes. Right now, it was brighter than the weather outside. Which wasn't saying much.

He phone buzzed. She unlocked the screen; message from Abigail.

Abigail Blackwell was, what most would consider, her best friend. She also worked at the RSC, in the Production Department. They had hit it off almost immediately when they had first met in the Dirty Duck pub. She had not gone to the pub voluntarily of course, her brother James had been visiting and had dragged her out on the last night of his trip to the UK. Abigail had bumped into her and spilled her Aperol Spritz on her new Converse.

White Converse. Orange drink.

Not a good combination. She had been terribly apologetic of course, and had insisted on buying her a new pair. Despite her protestations to the contrary.

"Abigail Blackwell" she said, holding out her hand.
"Kate Harrington" I said, shaking her hand shyly.
"Hey, don't you work in the curriculum office or something?" she asked.
"Yes, I do. And you?"
"Production" she said proudly. And rightly so, I thought. She was involved in staging all the plays, and got to meet all the actors. Lucky thing.
"Look, I'm really sorry about your shoes. Let me replace them, they're ruined"
"It'll wash out" I lied. It wouldn't. Definitely wouldn't.
"I insist" she smiled.
Why was she smiling at me? Girls usually smiled at James; he was super handsome, and girls loved him. But she hadn't even looked at him.
"This is my brother, James" I said, trying to focus her attention elsewhere.
"Hi James" she said politely. Then returned her attention to me. James said hi, and went off to the bar to get drinks, leaving me alone with her.
Drinks was a generous word; I didn't drink.
He would have a pint of course, but I'd have a soft drink. It hadn't always been like that of course; I had been introduced to social life at Uni, and had warmed to it slowly.
I had joined the others in my year group on nights out, and had gone to parties with my friend Sean. I had met him very early on in uni, and we had bonded for life.

There was no romantic interest of course; he was as gay as the day is long.
We had become close friends. The closest! He had accepted my quiet demeanour, and saw me for what I was; intelligent, clever, witty, loving, caring.
I had loved him, more than anything or anyone. As a friend of course. But still love. My entire life at Cambridge had revolved around him.
Until he hadn't come home one night. I had thought that he had maybe met someone or something, but found out the following morning that he had been killed by a car whilst walking home from the party.
Not the driver's fault; Sean had been drunk, and had staggered out into the road. The driver hadn't had the time to brake or avoid him. He had died instantly.
And so had my world. I was supposed to have gone to the party with him, but I wasn't feeling too good. That time of the month…
"You ok there?" Abigail asked.
"Pardon?"
"You looked lost"
"Oh, sorry"
"No worries. Look, I have to go. Give me your phone" She said, holding out her hand.
"What?"
"Your phone?"
Without thinking, I handed over my phone, and she sent herself a message on WhatsApp.
"Here" she said, handing it back to me. "I'll text you tomorrow, we'll go shopping"
"You really don't have to" I said.
"I want to. Speak tomorrow" She smiled, and left.

And so, Abigail Blackwell had entered my little life.
I stood alone outside, watching her descend the steps to the street below.
"Hey, got your drink" James said, reappearing.
"Thanks"
"Who's that? Someone from work?"
"It would appear so" I said.
"A friend?" He asked, hopefully.
"I don't know" I said truthfully.
"Don't do your usual" he warned.
"My usual?"
"You know, ignore people. Live a little sis, it's been a while"
He was right of course. Sean had died over three years ago now, and I knew I should move on. I just couldn't.
"I'll try" I lied.
"You need a life sis, and she seems nice"
"She does?"
"You don't think so? She seemed to like you"
"Why?"
"Why? Why not? You're not an unattractive woman"
"Sounds weird coming from you"
"Sounds weird saying it. But I'm being serious.
Sean has been gone for a while now, and you need somebody. You need a friend"
"I have friends" I protested.
"Work colleagues?"
"Still friends"
He rolled his eyes. "How about a real life friend?"
"I don't know"
"I do. Go shopping with her, have a bit of fun. What's the worst that could happen?"

"I hate shopping" I said. I did. I couldn't imagine anything more boring. And it was scary; so many people. I was an online shopper.
"Promise you'll go? For me?" he asked.
"Ugh, ok. I promise"
"Good. I'd hate to go home and leave you all alone again"
"I said I'll do it" I said.
"Ok, ok. Let's just drop it then shall we? When are you coming over this year?"
"Oh, I don't know yet. Maybe later on, when there's snow"
"Come for Christmas"
"What?"
"Christmas? Come over?"
"What about mum and dad?"
"What about them? I'm sure they can manage one Christmas without us. Besides, you'll get to meet Jane"
"Jane? Something you want to share?" I asked.
Who the hell was Jane??
"She's my... girlfriend I suppose"
"You *suppose*?"
"Well, we've only just started dating, so I don't really know yet"
I kissed his cheek "I'm really happy for you"
"I'm really happy for me too" he smiled.
He had been in a long-term relationship with the very popular Jennifer Langthorne before he had made the decision to move to America. That had not been part of her life plan; she envisaged marrying James and living in the country somewhere.
That being the case, she had dropped him like a brick.

He had been heartbroken. Still was probably. That was three years ago now also... How had he been able to move on but I hadn't? What the hell was wrong with me?

"It's been a while, I'm glad you found somebody new" I smiled.

"Thank you"

"What's she like?"

"Well, she's pretty..."

"Goes without saying. What is she like?"

"She's sporty. She runs, climbs, swims"

"Unlike you" I chuckled.

"Hey, I'll have you know I can run seven kilometres now. And I swim twice a week"

"Good for you" I smiled. "She's obviously good for you then"

"Yes, she is" he smiled.

I could tell he was totally smitten; he looked happy just thinking about her. I wish I had someone like that.

Oh wait, I did. Or used to at least. And now? It was just me and the cat.

"Hey, you know what? I'll let you buy me a drink" I said. Impulsive. Not my usual style.

"You will?"

"Yes, why the hell not"

"Ok" he said, looking surprised "And what would madame like to drink?"

"I'll try an Aperol spritz"

He smiled "Of course"

I stood alone for a while, feeling extremely self-conscious. James was my safety blanket, and now he was at the bar.

I looked around nervously, wondering what to do with myself. I must look like a complete nutjob.

I took my phone from my pocket, and pretended to be texting. In reality, I was reading a random Shakespeare sonnet. Anything to make myself look interesting.

Where was he? He'd been gone for ages. I could feel my heart rate increasing. I checked on my watch: 87. Calm down Kathrina. Calm. Calm.

"Sorry, bit of a queue"

Oh, thank God.

"No problem" I lied.

"Yes it was" he said. He knew me well. "We should have gone together"

"It's fine James" I said.

"What's your heart rate?"

"What?"

"Your heart rate, I know you check it all the time"

"Eighty seven"

"Let's drink this and go home" he said.

"Yes, I think I'd like that" I could have just quite happily have left the drink and gone home straight away. But, I felt I should drink it, for James' sake.

2. Waiting to happen.

I woke, as per usual, before the alarm went off. It was a stupendously irritating habit. I wished I could sleep in like normal people. My usual routine consisted of the following:

- Get up
- Shower
- Breakfast: Greek yoghurt/honey/raspberries
- Brush teeth
- Dress
- Hair/Makeup
- Leave for work.

There were no deviations from the plan today. I was out of the door within an hour, and made it into work exactly half an hour early, at 07.30. I had left James asleep in the spare bedroom; he wouldn't crawl out of bed for a few hours yet. We had said our goodbyes last night, and he would let himself out when he was ready to go. His plane was at three, so he had plenty of time. Outside the RSC, a few people milled around, standing out with their red lanyards. We all wore red lanyards, even to the pub, where it got us a discount of sorts. Plus, people liked wearing it to show off.
I parked my bike and locked it up. Right, time for coffee, then to work. I went to my usual place for coffee; Marco's Italian Deli. It was only a short walk away, and they served the best coffee around.

"Ah la bella signora Kate" he said, grinning.
"Morning Marco" I smiled.
"You like the usual?"
"Yes please"
"I make myself" he smiled, and worked the machine. When he had finished, he set the coffee on the counter and gave me his usual mischievous look. "Here you go, and a little treat for later" he smiled, bagging a freshly made pistachio cannoli.
"You spoil me" I smiled, playing for the coffee.
"You are good customer" he smiled "Have a good day"
"And you, thank you Marco"
"Ciao bella" he smiled theatrically.
I had been coming to Marco's for almost two years now, and he'd started giving me a free cannoli a few months ago. I wasn't about to complain; they were delicious.
I walked back to the RSC and went up to my office. The team were just arriving, and we had our usual morning huddle before getting to work.
Whilst I wasn't known for my public speaking, I could speak to my team without issues. They mostly consisted of students on work experience placement or on a gap year. We all got along nicely, and they knew their jobs pretty well, so there was little for me to involve myself with.
I sat at my computer and updated my notes for *As You Like It*, based on my having watching it the previous evening. It had been a half-hearted effort at best; I hadn't really been in the mood. The weather was foul, and so had been my mood. The fog had set in as soon as the first rain drops hit the window.

I salvaged what I could and saved my progress.
I was disappointed with myself.
My mood had dictated my work efforts.
Not that I was on the clock at home and feeling the pressure, I just watched to stay relevant and keep ahead of the game. And I enjoyed it. A lot.
However, I wasn't feeling it today.
Maybe a change of environment? I packed my laptop and was about to head out to Café Nero when my phone buzzed. A message? For me?
Probably James saying goodbye before his flight.
I picked up my phone and unlocked it. Three messages. One from James saying goodbye, one from mum asking why I never called, and one from… Abigail.
Hey, still up for shopping? Let me know when you finish, I'll be finishing at three.

Oh shit. I thought she'd forget, and I could just go on living my happy, quiet life. I *could* finish at three, I had plenty of annual leave left. But, did I *want* to? My heart was going like crazy. I was ridiculously nervous already. This wasn't good. I checked my bag, and to my relief found the emergency strip of Propranolol in there. Thank goodness. If there was ever an emergency, this was it. I took the pill, and a deep breath.
Calm down Kate, it's just a bloody message.
My thumbs hovered over the keyboard. Just type.
A polite "Thank you, but my shoes are really ok".
Yes, that would do right? I started typing, and was about to press Send when I remembered I'd promised James I would give it a go. Shit. I deleted the text.

Blank screen. What do I say? I had no idea.
Come on girl, this isn't difficult. What would a normal woman type? Sod it, I just typed a quick message and hit Send. Then I put the phone away quickly, as if not seeing her reply would make it better.
Seconds later the phone buzzed. I picked it up and stared at it. What if she said no? That is was all just a joke? That she'd been put up to it by her friends or something? For a laugh. I couldn't look. I put the phone back in my bag.
"Jenny, I'm heading out to Nero for a bit, change of scenery, you know?"
"Ok boss, no prob. I'll keep an eye on this riffraff"
Jenny was the longest serving member of my team, and as such had reached a level of unofficial second in-chargeness. She loved it, and the rest of the guys didn't mind at all. It was handy, as she could watch over the team whilst I slipped out if I felt down.
Right, time to go, get some air.
I picked up my bag and walked outside, into the sunlight. It was a busy day, and there were people everywhere. Not good.
It never ceased to amaze me how many people visited Stratford-upon-Avon. Though I shouldn't be so surprised I guess. It was the birthplace of Shakespeare after all. The RSC shop was rammed, as was the café.
I walked across the square and headed for Nero.
Not my preferred option, especially at this time of day. But, choices were limited.

I saw it from across the street. Shit. It's heaving. I put on my headphones and listened to an audiobook whilst standing in the queue.

My nerves were on edge, but the soothing tones of the narrator kept me sane. I got to the front and ordered a large Latte and a pain aux raisin to go. I waited patiently, trying to focus on the audiobook rather than the oppressive madness of the coffee shop. When my order was ready, I collected it and beat a hasty retreat. I walked along the river towards Holy Trinity Church. I'd go to my usual space in the shade, safely hidden amongst the grave stones.

The tourists generally refrained from wandering amongst the headstones, so it wasn't difficult to hide away. They were mostly interested in the church and Shakespeare's grave within.

Relieved, I sat in my safe place, next to Mary Allen Brasher, Born 1752, died 1804. Other details unknown.

"Hey Mary, how are you today? It's bloody crazy out there, you mind if I sit with you for a bit?"

She couldn't reply, obviously, but it felt respectful to ask. I sat back, and rested against her headstone. If she minded, she didn't say. Not that she could of course. I loved coming here, it was my go-to place for solitude. It was nice and cool under the trees, and all I could hear was the sound of birds tweeting and some geese honking loudly on the river. I sipped my coffee and ate my pastry. I sighed with relief. Peace at last.

The message. Was it from Abigail?

I should read it.

Shouldn't I?

Of course I should. I took the phone from my bag and unlocked it; one new message.
I opened it.
Hey, that's great. Meet you out front at three!
Was she being serious? Or was I going to turn up, and she wouldn't be there? Would they all be hiding, laughing at me from their concealment? What was I doing? I should have just said no. Idiot.
Too late now. If I didn't show, she'd come find me and that would only make it worse.
"Did you ever have problems like this Mary? I bet you did. I bet you had plenty of friends around you"
No response came. It never did.
Unless she was communicating through goose honks, which I doubted. Because that would be weird right?
I "Liked" the message, and put the phone away.
Three o'clock. It was now just before twelve; three hours to go. I was a bag of nerves already...
My heart was pounding like mad. I popped another pill from the strip and swallowed it down with a mouthful of coffee.
Then, I took a breath, pulled out my laptop and did some work.

At half past two, I was back at the office, standing in the toilets, staring at myself in the mirror. Jesus. What a sight. I was an absolute mess.
I fixed what little makeup I wore, and sorted my hair out. My hair was short. Ish. Blonde. Naturally so.

My brother said the short hair put men off as they'd all think I was a lezzer. I didn't care. I wasn't interested in men. Did that make me a lezzer? I didn't know. As far as I knew, I wasn't interested in women either. I just wasn't interested in anybody period. Was that weird? I was twenty seven years old, and had really only ever had one boyfriend. Mark Leicester, back in year six. We had kissed, but nothing more. But, he hadn't been satisfied with that. In fact, he had been a bit pushy, trying to force his hand under my jumper. I didn't like it, so broke up with him. He got angry, called me a dyke, and stormed off. Telling everyone I was a frigid lesbian. Great. Now they all thought I was a lesbian, just because I didn't put out. How narrow minded these people were. I couldn't wait to get out of that school. It had been a nightmare from start to finish.
Anyway, hair. Get on with it.
Well, nothing much I can do with it. It'll just have to do. I sprayed a little perfume. A little, not too much.
Didn't want to give her the wrong idea.
My heart had slowed. The pill was working. Should I take another, just to be sure? No. I'd had two already. I just needed to calm myself. I headed upstairs to speak to the team before I left for the day.
The guys had been busy on finalising the Chinese language curriculum we had been painstakingly working on for the last three months.
It was almost ready, and just needed my approvals.
I took the USB drive from Jenny and promised I would go through the files this evening.
And I would. Probably over dinner. Just me and the cat.

I left them to it and headed out. It was only ten to three, but I didn't want to be late. Besides, if I was early, I might spot the setup. It there was one.

I sat on the bench next to the statue of the Bard and waited. Nervously. Anxiously.

There she was, out front, on the steps. I checked my watch; two minutes to three.

I sat for a minute, just observing.

I wanted to make sure it wasn't a setup. She took her phone from her pocket and typed out a message.

A second later, my phone buzzed.

Outside. Ready when you are.

Oh God. It wasn't a joke; it was real. Shit, shit, shit. My heart tried its best to accelerate, but the medication prevented it from doing so. Thankfully.

I put my phone away and walked over.

This was really happening.

Time to put on the mask.

3. She Chameleon.

I slowly walked up the steps to the front entrance. Abigail was standing with her back to me, looking inside, waiting for me to appear.
"Hey" I said, making her jump a little.
"Jesus" she chuckled "You made me jump. I thought you were still inside"
"I was a little early, sorry"
"No, it's fine" she smiled "Ready?"
"Yep" I smiled.
"Cool, let's go then"
We walked along, no words were spoken. I was desperately trying to think of something to say, but my mind wouldn't allow it. I was terrible at his. Jesus. Why?
"I'm sorry about your shoes" she said, breaking the silence "They looked new"
"Oh, I'd had them for a while, that's why I wasn't too bothered" I said, greatly relieved that she'd been the one to break the silence; I was getting uncomfortable. And I'm sure she was too.
She eyed me suspiciously "Are you sure? They looked brand new?"
Ah. How could I explain this? I look after my stuff. I cleaned the shoes after each outing, hence they were still pristine. They were about six months old. There were no ways I could think of to explain that without sounding boring and completely idiotic.

"A couple of weeks maybe" I smiled "I hadn't had a chance to wear them out"
"Ah, I see. Well, let's go find some replacements shall we?"
We walked off into the town centre, in search of a shoe shop. Trouble was, there weren't many of those in Stratford. I'd bought the shoes online, as I did everything. This was going to end in failure.
"So, how long have you worked at the RSC?" she asked as we walked. She knew this already. We'd talked about work in the pub that night. Maybe she'd forgotten. Or, maybe, this is what normal people did.
"About two years. You?"
"Same. Weird that we haven't seen each other around before. Well, I haven't seen you around at least"
"I don't tend to socialise much" I said before I could stop myself. Idiot! Why would you say that?
"You don't?" she asked.
Shit. Now I would have to explain. Good work Kate…
"I, erm, don't do well around people"
"Oh, I see. Well, you seem to be doing fine just now" she smiled.
That's because I'm on pills and pretending, I thought.
"I'm having one of my good days" I explained. Which was true I suppose. I was.
"Oh" she smiled "Lucky for me"
"I didn't mean it in a bad way" I added hastily.
"Relax, I didn't take it in a bad way. Why would I?" she smiled.
We walked through Henley Street, but there weren't any shops that sold sports shoes. I knew this, of course, which is why I bought them online.

"Well, I can't see anywhere to get your shoes, sorry. Fancy a coffee? I can buy them online later"
"Coffee sounds good" I smiled "Please don't worry about the shoes. I have plenty of them"
Please don't argue the point, please don't argue the point. Please.
"If you're sure?" she asked.
"I'm sure" I smiled "I have plenty of shoes"
We walked back up the street and went into Nero. It was emptier than it had been when I was here earlier and we found a table quite easily.
"Latte?" she asked.
How did she know that I drank latte?
"Yes" I said. "How did you know?"
"It's not magic. Just a lucky guess. Most people drink latte's"
"Ah, I see" She wasn't a mind reader. Relief.
"Be right back" she smiled.
She got up and went to the counter.
I looked around, and wished I could put my headphones on. It was super noisy with people chatting. What do people find to talk about? They were all talking over each other, it was chaos. I tried to listen, but it was impossible to single out a conversation.
Conversation. It had never been my strong point. Ever. I was a hell of a listener though.
"I brought sugar, but I guess you don't take any"
"I don't"
"You don't look like you do" she said, sitting down.
What did that mean? Do I look like a non-sugar-in-coffee muppet? Did I look like I was on a diet?

Was I too thin? Shit. Was that it? She thinks I'm too thin! Great.

She could obviously see my confusion, as she quickly added "You're naturally slim, you lucky thing"

Not sure why she would say that, she wasn't exactly overweight. In fact, I'd swear we were the same size. Except for our busts maybe. Hers was considerably larger than mine. Not that I had been staring. Oh shit. What if she thinks I stare? Calm down.

"Genes" I said. Which was true enough. "I also don't eat rubbish, and exercise, I guess that helps too"

"Ah! Lucky girl. I have to work hard at it"

"Well, you're doing a good job"

"Oh, thank you" she said, seemingly surprised.

She was obviously pleased that I had noticed. I had, but it's not like I had checked her out in detail and made a judgement. She just looked the same as me. Please don't think I've been staring.

"I have to be careful about what I eat and drink. I also have to go to the gym every day. Do you work out?"

"I cycle to work, and walk a lot, occasional bit of running. But I don't go to the gym"

"You cycle in this chaos?"

"It's an eight minute ride, quiet roads" I explained.

"You live nearby?"

"Over in Tiddington"

"You rent a flat there? I rent in the town, small place up on Evesham Road"

"I, erm, live in a house. Well, a bungalow to be precise"

"Cool. You share?"

"No, I live alone"

"You rent a house to yourself?" she asked, confused.

"Erm, no, I bought it"
"Oh my God! You got a mortgage? Wow, that's great. Good for you. I haven't a chance"
"No, I bought it. No mortgage"
She looked at me, puzzled. "Are you rich?"
"Not particularly" Why would she think that? Ah. She wants an explanation you moron.
"I inherited some money a few years ago" I said.
"Ooh, nice. Wish there was money in my family"
"I was lucky"
"I'll say" She looked at me for a moment, then said "You want to get out of here?"
"What?"
"I can see how uncomfortable you are. It's the noise isn't it?"
"I'm ok" I said, unconvincingly.
She stood and walked over to the counter. When she returned, she had two takeaway cups in her hands. She deftly poured our drinks into them, without spilling a drop.
"Let's get out of here" she smiled.
We walked out into the sunshine, and stood for a moment outside the coffee shop, wondering where to go. She looked at me, expectantly.
"You have somewhere you go?" she asked.
"Somewhere I go?"
"A quiet place. Is there a quiet place you go when it all gets too much?"
"Yes"
"Let's go there"

The walk to the graveyard took about ten minutes, during which time we talked about work. Her job sounded absolutely fascinating, making me slightly jealous. She was heavily involved in the Company's next production, *Macbeth*, which was due to run from October until January.
She told me they were still busy casting the roles, but that it had sold out completely already.
"Wow, that's impressive" I said.
"People love *Macbeth*"
"It is what most would consider the quintessential Shakespeare play" I said.
"I'll take your word for it" she smiled.
"Over this way" I said, as we walked into the church grounds.
She followed me through the maze of headstones, and I was afraid she'd make a comment about me being weird for sitting in a graveyard. But, she didn't.
"This is where I come" I said as we reached Mary's grave. "Her name was Mary Allen Brasher"
She looked around "Nice spot. Mary Allen Brasher? Family?" she asked.
I shook my head "I don't know who she is"
We sat down, and enjoyed the silence for a moment.
"Can I ask something?" I asked.
"Sure" she smiled.
"Why are you here?"
She looked confused. "Why am I here?"
I instantly regretted asking. Jesus. Why?
"I'm sorry, that was a stupid question"
"It's only a stupid question if you don't explain your reasoning" she said kindly.

"I'm not very good with people" I said.
"We've established that already" she smiled.
"Yes, I guess so. I suppose it's just a question that means are you here because of me, or because of James?"
"James?" she looked confused.
"My brother. You met him at the pub, remember?"
"Oh, yes. Why would I be here because of him?"
"Girls tend to like him" I explained.
"No. I'm not here because of James" she said, shaking her head slowly.
That meant she was here for me. I didn't know if that was scarier or not. Yes, definitely scarier. By miles.
"Ah" I said, still unsure. Had I upset her? Shit.
"Hey, I'm not angry or anything. Just a bit confused. You obviously have self-image problems"
"Yes, I suppose I do. I don't make friends easily"
"Are we friends?" she asked, looking sceptical.
"What? I…"
"Kidding. I'd like to be your friend though. If that's ok?"
"Yes" I said, almost too quickly.
"Good. Just so you know, I'm not interested in your brother"
"He's taken anyway apparently" I said.
"I should hope so, he's a good looking guy"
"You have a boyfriend?"
Boyfriend? What are you? Like twelve? I chastised myself for being so childish. For God's sake.
"Me? No" she laughed.
What was so funny? Was it me? Was she mocking me?
"That's funny?" I asked.
"Sorry. No, I, erm, I'm not into men" she explained.

"Oh, I see" I said, and blushed.
"Is that going to be an issue?" she asked, worried.
"What? No, of course not" Wasn't it? Wasn't it?
"I do just want to be your friend" she said, as if trying to reassure me.
"I'm not sure I'm the best person to be friends with" I said "I have... issues"
"We all have issues" she chuckled, then turned serious again "Look, I can tell you have anxiety issues. Loud noises, crowds. Not your thing. I get it. I don't mind"
"You sure?"
"Of course. Why don't you tell me about yourself Kate Harrington?"
"Me? Well, there's not really much to tell" I lied.
"I doubt that very much" she smiled "Go on, try it"
"Ok. Well, my name you know I suppose. I'm twenty seven, from Kennington originally"
"Kennington? Where's that?"
"Oxford"
"Ah, I see"
"I went to school in Oxford, then onto uni at Cambridge. From there, I found myself here doing work experience at the RSC. I liked it, so applied for a more permanent position"
"You're from Oxford, but went to Cambridge?"
I laughed "Yes, much to my mother's chagrin. She went to Oxford, and had really wanted me to follow in her footsteps"
"But you rebelled?"
"Yes, I guess so"
"Good for you" she smiled.

"I guess I just wanted to get away from home, stand on my own two feet"
"Kate… Catherine?"
"Kathrina, with a K"
"That sounds Russian" she said.
"Swedish actually"
"Your parents are Swedish?"
"Just my mother"
"That explains the figure and the hair" she smiled.
"Yes, I guess it does"
"What do your parents do?"
"Dad is a Barrister, and mum a Psychologist"
"That explains the money" she chuckled.
"They live well, but that's not where I got the money for the house. My nan won the money in the lottery"
"Wow! That's amazing. I've never met anyone that's won more than a tenner on the lottery. She must have won big"
"Yes, she did"
"That's a good-news story" she smiled. "How was your time at uni?"
"It was… ok I suppose. For the most part" I said quietly.
"Oh, I'm sorry. I didn't mean to pry"
"No, it's fine. James says I should talk about it more, makes it better apparently" I laughed nervously. "I had a friend, Sean. We were close. Very close. We used to do everything together, parties, studies, travel. Hard to believe, I know, but I wasn't always like this"
"What happened?" she asked.
"We were supposed to go to this party together, but I wasn't feeling too well. Time of the month, you know… Anyway, he went alone, got drunk, and walked home.

They think he staggered out into the road, straight into the path of a car. He was killed instantly"
"Oh my God, I'm so sorry" she said, putting her hand on mine. A tiny spark of electricity passed through me as she did so. It was unexpected, and I almost pulled my hand away. But, I didn't.
"It's fine" I lied "It was three years ago now. I felt terribly guilty for like the longest time. I should have been there, then he'd still be here"
"I can imagine that, but you shouldn't blame yourself"
"I know that now" I lied again "But then... it was different. I stopped drinking, stopped going out. I hid away from the world"
"You're still hiding?" she asked.
That made me think for a moment. Was I? I guessed so. I still didn't go out, and I definitely hid away from the world. Would it make me look like an idiot if I said yes? It was obvious though surely? Just tell the truth.
"Yes" I said, then hastily added "But I had a drink the other night. At the pub. After you'd left. I tried an Aperol Spritz"
She laughed "Good girl. Did you like it?"
"Yes, I think I did" It wasn't a lie, I had.
"Good. Now I know what to buy you when we go out at least"
"Go out?" I asked, alarmed.
"Yes. It's my birthday on Saturday"
"Oh, I don't know" I said, nervously.
"Look. The work thing is tomorrow night. Saturday night will just be you and me. Promise."
"Like a date?" I asked.

"Like two friends, going out, having a laugh" she corrected.

This was escalating a little too quickly for my liking. It was bad enough sitting here with her, let alone a night out.

"You said you're still hiding away from the world. Let me help you come back into the light"

"I..."

"Look, I won't make a pass at you, if that's what you're worried about"

"No, it's not that. Let me think about it?"

"Thinking is dangerous" she said "Gives your mind time to conjure up reasons why you shouldn't do something"

"Wow. You sound like my mother" I said.

"Oh God" she laughed "Do I? I'm so sorry"

I could feel myself getting closer and closer to saying no, so I just blurted out "Ok, I'll come"

She looked surprised "You will?"

"Yes. That's good isn't it?"

My turn to look confused. I thought that was what she wanted me to say? Ugh. Did I get it wrong again?

"Yes it is" she smiled. "Right, I have to get going sorry, my turn to cook tonight"

"You live in shared accommodation?"

"Yes, there's three of us"

"Sounds fun" I lied.

"Can be. Sometimes not quite so much"

"Ok, cool. I'll see you Saturday then" I said.

"What? I thought we could do lunch tomorrow"

"Oh, yeah, sure" I said. Lunch? What are you thinking? You don't do lunch. "Only..."

"Yes?"
"I don't really do lunch"
"That explains the skinniness even more" she smiled, then said "Breakfast then?"
"Yes, that would be nice" I said, relieved.
"Cool. I'll meet you outside work at seven?"
"Perfect"
"Good. In the meantime, you have my number, don't be a stranger" she winked.
"What? Oh, sure" I said.
"Oh, one more thing" she said "Stand up"
I did so, and she put her arm around me. "Picture"
We did a selfie, and I tried my best to look natural. She looked at her phone, smiled and walked back in the direction of the town centre, leaving me alone with Mary.
"What do you think Mary?" I asked. "Did I make an idiot out of myself? I feel like I did. Silence is golden eh? See you tomorrow"
I got up, and walked back to work to retrieve my bike.

4. Where Paranoia Roams.

I cycled home and had a long bath, worrying about going out on Saturday.
Going out was bad enough, but going out with Abigail? Not that it was bad per se, just nerve wracking.
What should I wear? Oh God, my wardrobe choices were extremely limited. My usual combination of jeans and band t-shirt didn't seem appropriate. A dress then?
Those were my only two options. I didn't wear "Athleisure", except if I was running, and didn't own any skirts.
I didn't like the way men looked at me when I wore tight or revealing clothing, so everything I owned was baggy.
A dress then. Those at least made me look half decent. And girly. Ugh, I hated this.
I rinsed the conditioner from my hair and got out of the bath, then wrapped myself in a huge towel and went to my bedroom.
The cat was sitting on the bed, watching me dry off and put my pyjamas on. She looked at me in her usual judgemental way. She soon scarpered though when I turned on the hairdryer.
"Scaredy cat!" I shouted after her.
After drying my hair, I went back to the bathroom and cleaned the bath. As I did so, the worries re-surfaced; should I go? If so, which dress should I wear? I had no idea.

I went back to the bedroom and went through the dresses in my wardrobe.

Most were floral and summery. And then I had two dresses that Sean had made me buy; a black one, and a pale grey one. They were both hideously tight and short, and I hadn't worn them since he'd died. To think I used to wear them out! Jesus. I took them from the hanger, folded them, and put them in a plastic bag; they were headed for the charity shop. I was never going to wear them again. That Kate was thankfully gone.

Choices. My enemy. I placed the remaining dresses on the bed. Colour choices; red, green, blue, orange, and grey. I stared at them for ages, making pro and con lists for each one in my mind.

An idea came to me. I knew what normal women did! I picked up my phone and sent a load of pictures to Abigail.

Seconds later, she replied; the picture we'd taken at the graveyard. Oh my God, I looked so awkward. Yet happy.

My phone buzzed again; she replied: *Blue. Deffo. X*

What was with the kiss? No, let's not over-analyse. It's just something else normal women did.

The blue dress was something I'd bought on impulse after seeing Holly Willoughby wearing it on the TV. According to Evoke, it was from La Redoute, which was a bonus as it was online. And at only £40, it was worth a gamble, and it had paid off by the look of it.

Next problem; feet. I had some skin coloured sandals that looked good with it. Toes then. I'd have to paint my nails. Which meant doing my finger nails too, as my normal black didn't go with blue very well. What colour then? Ugh. It was never ending. I'd worry about that tomorrow. I hung the dresses back in the wardrobe, got my clothes ready for work tomorrow, and went to watch some TV.

The following morning, I was woken by the alarm clock. "What?" I said aloud, confused.
I usually woke up before the alarm! I focussed on the time, and saw it was six o'clock. Of course.
I remembered I had set it a bit earlier as I was meeting Abigail for breakfast.
Shit! I was meeting Abigail for breakfast! My stomach dropped and I was instantly a bag of nerves.
Calm down. Take a tablet, have a shower, and just go to work as per normal. It's just breakfast for God's sake, control yourself. Easier said than done.
I took a tablet, and had a quick shower, then completed the rest of my routine and rode my bike into work.
I got about halfway there when I started worrying about what I was wearing today. Jeans, t-shirt, and trainers. Not exactly glam.
Shit. What if she thought I was a tramp? Too late to change now. Just keep going.
I approached the RSC slowly, trying to spot her before she saw me, so I could see what she was wearing.
To my relief, she was wearing jeans and a t-shirt. Not a band t-shirt, but a Levi's one.
Her long brown hair was in a ponytail, and she was wearing tight, but flattering jeans. She looked nice.
And I looked like a lesbian. Genius.

"Morning" I said, stopping in front of her.
"Morning" she smiled.
"I'll just go get rid of the bike, be right back"
"Ok, I'll be here"
I rode off round the corner and locked up my bike. I clipped my helmet to my bag and walked back.
"Cool tee" she said as I walked up.
I was instantly self-conscious. Was she taking the piss or being serious?
"I saw them at the O2 last year" she said, reassuring me.
"Cool" I smiled "Lucky you"
I was wearing my Killers 2015 Tour t-shirt. I'd bought it when I went to see them in Cardiff ten years ago.
"2015 tour? Showing your age there aren't you?"
Shit. I realised I had no idea how old she was. What if she was much younger than me? Oh God. But then, she knew how old I was already. I had told her yesterday, and she hadn't run a mile.
"I was seventeen" I said, uneasily.
"I was sixteen" she smiled "Too young to go. My parents didn't let me go to concerts till I was eighteen"
"Ah, I see. I was lucky, I went with James. He's a year older" My relief was immense. She was only a year younger than me.
"Good for you" she smiled. "Where are we headed?"
"Marco's?"
"Where is that?"
"This way" I said, leading the way.
We walked down the steps and crossed the road.
"Whereabouts is this place?" she asked as we walked.
"Church Street"

"Really? I've never noticed it before"

"It's not a big place, probably why"

We turned into Church Street and walked on past the alms houses.

"It's just here opposite the Council Offices" I said.

"Oh wow" she said "Never noticed it"

We walked in, and I was greeted by Marco in his usual flamboyant Italian manner.

"Ah signora Kate, you are early today" he smiled.

"Morning Marco. Yes, I am. I've brought a friend for breakfast"

"A friend?" he asked, waiting for an introduction.

"Marco, This is Abigail, we work together"

"Another beautiful lady to brighten my day" he smiled.

"Morning, nice to meet you" Abigail said.

"My lucky day!" he said "Two beautiful ladies. Sit, sit. I make you coffee"

Without asking what she wanted, he went off to work his machine.

"He's a charmer" Abigail said, leaning in close.

"He's harmless. And his coffee is the best"

He returned a minute or so later.

"Cappuccino's for my beautiful guests" he smiled, placing the cups on the table.

"Thank you Marco, what do your recommend for breakfast?"

"I have pastries, or I can do English breakfast"

I looked at Abigail.

"Oh, erm. Scrambled eggs on toast?" she asked.

"My speciality" he smiled proudly.

"I'll have the same" I said.

"Coming right up"

He disappeared out to the kitchen and got to work.
"You mind a cappuccino?" I asked. I was instantly paranoid. What if she didn't? Oh God.
"No, not at all" she assured me. Relief.
"He's Italian, he'll only serve cappuccino's in the mornings, it's traditional" I explained.
"I like cappuccino's" she smiled. "This place is nice, how long have you been coming here?"
"Oh, about two years now"
"I can tell. You're very at ease with him"
"He's lovely. It took a while for me to talk to him, it all happened gradually"
"It's a lovely place"
"It's quiet" I smiled.
"Yes. It is. I liked your dress by the way" she said.
"Oh, thank you. Something I bought a while back but haven't worn"
"It's very pretty. I'm sure you'll look fantastic in it"
"Thank you" I said, blushing.
Fortunately, Marco came to the rescue. "Ah, here we go. Breakfast for my bella signoras"
"Thanks Marco" I said.
"You enjoy" he smiled, and left us to it.
"Oh my God, this is lush" Abigail said, with a mouthful of eggs.
"Yeah, I know" I said.
"I'm guessing everything here is awesome?" she asked.
"Yes, the pastries are good, the sandwiches, everything. It's all freshly made"
"Hmmm, good to know"
We finished our breakfast, and I paid Marco before Abigail could reach into her bag.

"My treat" I said.
Marco thanked me, and handed me a paper bag.
"For later" he winked. Two cannoli.
"You're a star" I said, and kissed his cheek.
Jesus! What are you doing? That's not you!
He looked as surprised as I was, but said nothing.
We left him standing behind the counter, still trying to process what had just happened.
"What's in the bag?" Abigail asked as we walked back to work.
"Pistachio cannoli. I get one free very day"
"Wow, lucky you. He must have a soft spot for you"
"I guess" I said, then hastily added "Wait, I don't usually kiss his cheek"
Oh God, what had I done? That was so not me. What must she think?
She laughed "I can tell. It's a sign"
"Of?"
"You emerging into the light"

I didn't see Abigail for the rest of the day, which wasn't unusual I guess. I just found myself missing her.
I thought I caught a glimpse of her and a group of people heading off towards the Dirty Duck when I unlocked my bike.
Why was I looking out for her? Did I fancy her? No, it was just what friends do. What normal women do, remember?
I put on my helmet and cycled home, self-doubt running freely through my mind.
In order to clear my head of paranoid thoughts, I went out for a run before dinner. I was a beautiful evening,

and I decided to run the 5k Parkrun course around the recreation grounds.

Today, men staring at me as I ran past them didn't seem to bother me for some reason. I ignored their stares, and ran around lost in my own little world. What was going on with me?

After I got back home, I checked my run on the Garmin app on my phone. Not too bad.

I took the usual picture of my shoes, never my face, added the stats on the app, and uploaded it to my Instagram. I had four followers on my Instagram; mum, dad, James, and Sean.

Ooh, there was a message from Abigail. My heart rate increased instantly.

I opened it; it was a picture of her in the pub, the caption read: *Wish you were here. x*

I smiled. Yeah, if only I was that confident.

After a long hot shower, I made some salad for dinner and re-watched *As You Like It*, determined to make better notes this time.

5. Apprentice Seductress.

Saturday. A day to myself. Alone with my thoughts. Not a particularly good thing.
By lunchtime, I had done my shopping (online of course), cleaned the house, and done my laundry, ironing, and a bit of gardening.
I was pooped. I got a cold glass of water and sat out in the back garden. I lay back and was going to allow myself to fall asleep when my phone rang.
I picked it up and stared at it like one would a live hand grenade.
Oh. My Mother. Dammit.
"Hey mum"
"Oh, hello Kathrina. Thought I'd call you seen as I'd never hear your voice otherwise"
"Thanks"
If there was anyone that should understand what I'd gone through, and why I was the way I was, it should be my mother, the psychologist.
But, she didn't. Or, to be more precise, she never took the time to find out. And I didn't want to be analysed by my own mother.
"Well, how are you?" she asked, impatiently.
"I'm fine mum"
"Did you have a nice time with your brother?"
"Yes, it was good"
"Good"
Silence. Ugh. She was purposely waiting for me to say something. She did this all the time.

"How are you and dad?" I asked, giving her exactly what she'd wanted.

"We're good. Your father is off to London for a couple of days, so I'm alone this weekend"

I knew what she wanted; me to come to home for the weekend to spend time with her.

Silence.

"Kathrina, I wish you would speak to someone. I can recommend a good friend of mine if you won't speak to me"

Counselling, again. She was like a broken record.

"I'm going out tonight" I said.

"Really Kathrina, you don't have to invent excuses to not come here"

"Mum, I'm going out tonight. It's Abigail's birthday"

"Abigail? Who's Abigail?"

"A friend"

There was silence, but I could hear enough to know she was crying. Shit.

"Mum, you ok?" I asked.

"You made a friend?" she asked, between sobs.

"Yes mum. She's nice. We went shopping Thursday, then had breakfast yesterday"

"Oh!" she exclaimed "I'm so happy for you"

More like happy for yourself, I thought.

"Hang on" I said, then sent her the selfie of Abigail and Myself as proof. "Check your messages"

There was silence for a while whilst she checked the picture.

"Oh my God Kathrina, you look so happy"

"Thank you mother"

"Your friend is pretty"

"Yes"
"You look good together"
"What? No, mum, it's not like that"
"This is the 21st century Kathrina, it's nothing to be ashamed of"
"It's not like that mum"
"Ok, ok, if you say so"
Something had changed; my mother was being nice to me. Caring. Almost like... a mother.
"Where are you going? The Black Swan?"
I rolled my eyes "The Dirty duck"
She refused to say the name, it sounded far too common for her liking. The pub was weird in a way that it had two names; The Dirty Duck, and The Black Swan.
One for the commoners, one for the posh people I supposed. And my mother was most definitely posh people.
"I had a drink"
There was another silence.
"Just the one" I added, trying to lessen the shock.
"What's happening to you?" she asked, still crying.
"What do you mean?" I asked, instantly worried.
"You're moving on. Finally"
"I guess so" I lied.
"I'm so proud. And happy for you"
"Thanks mum"
"What are you wearing tonight?"
"A dress mum" I reassured her.
"Oh, I didn't mean..."
"It's fine mum' I'll send you a picture before I head out"

"That would be lovely" She sounded dead proud.
"Mum?"
"Yes?"
"What colour should I do my nails for a blue dress?"
"Light pink. Nothing bold"
"Thanks"
"Good luck, she looks lovely"
"Thanks mum. It's not like that"
"Love you"
She never said that...
"Love you too mum"
I dialled off.

I tried in vain to fall asleep in the garden after the call. Various things were going through my mind though.
My mother had cried. Cried. Jesus. She never cried. I know they were tears of happiness, but wasn't sure who she was happy for.
And her tone. Her tone had changed completely. It reminded me of... Of the way we'd talked before Sean had died. When I had been normal in her eyes.
Why did everyone think I was gay? Even my own mother. For God's sake.
She had me doubting myself now. No. There were no feelings like that in my mind. At all.
So why was I making such an effort? I had even laid out my best white bra and pants set.
I just wanted to look nice. Nothing wrong with that.
I wasn't doing it for Abigail. I was doing it for myself. Wasn't I?
I picked up my phone and text James: Hey, you think I'm gay?

I went inside and made a sandwich. When I returned, he'd text back.
Would it be so wrong if you were?
That's not what I asked dimwit.
What other people think isn't important. What do you think?
I don't know. Even mum thinks I am.
Mum? How so?
I sent her a picture of me and Abigail
Show me
Sent
Jesus Kate, you look radiant
Radiant? Does that translate as gay?
That's for you to discover for yourself
Thanks for nothing, muppet
It's your life sis, you'll work it out. You look good together though
Moron. Have a good weekend
And you

James was his usual vague, useless self. For someone supposedly super-intelligent, he lacked any form of common sense. That was a lie of course, he was super savvy in everything. He was just teasing me.
I went inside, threw my phone on the kitchen table, and went up for a shower. So much to do. I was wearing a dress, that meant I had to do my legs. After a very painful epilation, I sat at my little makeup table and removed the black polish from my fingernails. Looking through my little collection of nail varnish, I found the lightest pink I had. It was the only pink I had. I put some music on, and did my nails.

The soothing tones of Bach's cello suite in G major lightened my mood, and made me forget about my family questioning my sexuality for a while.
I lay back on the bed whilst my nails dried, and stared up at the ceiling for a while.
Was this really a good idea? What if she didn't turn up? What if it was all an elaborate joke?
What if... what if... Stop it already!
Once my nails had dried, I moved on to my hair.
Not that there was much I could do with it mind. It was short. Too short perhaps. It had seemed like a good idea at the time, and even more so because I knew it would piss my mother off. She had complained bitterly for ages after, unable to understand why I would cut off my beautiful long hair. She didn't understand that I just wanted to be someone else, and that necessitated a change in hairstyle.
Looking at it in the mirror now, I wanted it to grow back. Instantly.
Sadly, that wasn't going to happen, so I did the best I could.
Hair: done.
Nails: done.
Clothes time.
I took the dress from the wardrobe and hung it on the door. My underwear was on the bed. Was it too much? I could just wear the usual plain cotton.
I decided to try both.
I put on my trusty favourite cotton set and looked at myself in the mirror.
Looked fine.

Time to check the other. Stupidly, I already knew what the result was going to be…
I looked in the mirror. Shit. It was like night and day. The lacy white set made me look sexy, made me feel sexy too. I looked far better. My small-ish boobs looked far more impressive in the pushy up bra than they did in the cotton one.
Dammit. I decided to keep the lacy set on, as they made me feel better about myself.
Besides, it wasn't like anyone was going to see me in it.
I took the dress from the hanger and put it on. My God.
I looked nice.
No, I looked fantastic.
Happy, I sat down and did my makeup. I felt good about myself. For the first time in a long time.
Once I was done with the makeup, I took a picture for my mother. I knew it would make her cry.

Oh my God Kathrina, you look beautiful. X

What's with the kiss? Jesus, she'd lost it completely now. I could imagine her at the other end, tears dripping onto her phone screen as she stared at my picture, full of maternal pride. And relief. Mostly relief.
A message popped up as I was replying to mum; Abigail.
Quickly, I hit send and checked; hopefully, it wasn't a cancellation.
Hey, just checking; we did say seven right?
Yes, we did.
Cool. How's the dress looking?

It looks ok I guess.
You're so modest, I bet it looks fantastic.
I guess you'll find out later
Looking forward to it. X

I guess you'll find out later???
What the hell was that all about??
What was happening to me?
Jesus. Calm down. But I was calm. I checked my heartrate on my watch: 72.
A bit high, but not crazy. And I hadn't even taken a pill. I definitely would before heading out. There was no way I was going without my safety blanket.
I applied a little antiperspirant to my underarms, sprayed on some perfume, the expensive French one, and slipped into my sandals.
I was ready.

6. Unleashing the Stranger from a Kiss.

I took my safety pill and left the house. The taxi had waited patiently for me to emerge from the sanctity of my home.
I got in, and he confirmed the address.
"Dirty duck, right my Love?"
"Yes please"
He nodded, and drove. Love? Jesus. She normally struggled to get a simple response, let alone be called *love*.
Must be the new look. New look? Is that what this was? I doubted it. Tomorrow I'd be back in jeans and a tee. But, I supposed for tonight, this *was* it, and I was going to bloody well enjoy it.
The drive took about five minutes, and cost almost £15. Christ, I'll walk next time.
I thanked him, and got out. I stood on the pavement, and stared up at the pub; it was busy. Shit, shit, shit.
I took a breath, and walked up the narrow steps. Panic tried to strike as I did so, but I managed to keep it in check. I stood at the top of the steps, looking around the small terrace, no sign of Abigail. Oh no. What if…?
"Oh my God"
It was her. She was coming out from the bar, holding two drinks.
"You look beautiful" she said, aghast.
"Oh, thanks" I said coyly. "You look amazing"

She did. She was also wearing a dress.
Hers was light green, which went well with her hair, which hung loose over her shoulders.
Her nails were painted a faded tint of orange, and her makeup was understated, but perfect.
"You're staring" she said.
"So are you" I said.
"I have a table, over in the corner there"
We ducked under the tree, and sat in the corner. She had reserved an outside table? I thought that was impossible?
She put the drinks down, and I hugged her "Happy Birthday"
"Thank you" she smiled "I, erm, got you an Aperol Spritz"
"Perfect" I smiled.
We sat down, and toasted.
"Another year older" she said, holding up her glass.
"Like a fine wine" I added.
We touched glasses and sipped our drinks.
"I was afraid you weren't going to come" she said.
"Me too"
"But, you did"
"Apparently so"
"You look amazing Kate"
"So do you"
"I doubt that, but thank you. Is that Chanel I smell?"
"Yes" I said, embarrassed.
"I'm flattered, you broke out the good stuff"
"Doesn't happen often"
"I should hope not, seeing as it costs a fortune"
"It's not that bad really"

"For you maybe"
"You like it?"
"Who doesn't?"
"Twenty seven today eh?"
"Yes"
"We're the same age" I smiled.
"For how long?"
"Are you trying to find out when my birthday is?"
"I suppose I am" she smiled.
"Ninth of October"
"I see, not long then"
"No, edging ever closer to thirty"
"You don't look it"
"Those Swedish genes" I smiled.
"Lucky you"
"You don't look a day over twenty seven" I said.
"Charming!"
"I'm kidding. You look younger than me. I actually thought you were about twenty one or something"
"That's better" she smiled.
"I sent my mother that picture of us"
"And?"
"She cried"
"Jesus, it wasn't that bad was it?"
"She cried from happiness"
"Oh, I see. Well, that's good isn't it?"
"I suppose. She thinks we're an item"
She laughed. Why laugh? Was the idea so funny?
"Sorry" she said, holding up a hand "That was awful of me"
"I thought you were laughing because my family think I'm gay" I said.

"Your family?"
"My brother too"
"Why would they think that? Based on one photograph?"
I shrugged. "Dunno, I guess"
"When was your last relationship?"
"Define relationship"
"Something more than friends"
"Mark Leicester, year six"
She almost spat out her drink "Year six?? Jesus"
"Well, I suppose I loved Sean, but that was different"
"How so?"
"He was as gay as they get"
"I see" she chuckled. "So, nothing at all?"
"No, I guess not. You?"
"Me? Wow. Erm, a couple I guess. I met someone at uni, Janet. It lasted a few months. I thought we had a connection, but I was wrong. Since then? A one night stand with a girl I share the flat with. Nothing much happened really, but I still regret it. Bit awkward and all that"
"I can imagine" I laughed.
She stirred her drink with her straw, was she feeling uncomfortable? Shit. Talk! Ask questions!
"Tell me about yourself" I said, changing the subject.
"My turn eh? Very well. I'm from Salisbury originally. Went to school there, then uni in Southampton, Theatre Production. After uni, I worked at a few theatres before landing the job at the RSC two years ago. I live in the town with a couple of others. My dad works for the council, and my mum has her own business"

"Ooh, what kind of business?" I asked.
"She looks after people's cats when they're away on holiday" she said, seemingly embarrassed. She looked like she regretted telling me.
"Oh my God, I love cats" I said, clapping my hands together.
"You do?" she asked, a glimmer of happiness returning to her beautiful eyes.
"Yes, I have a tabby called Tabitha"
"Tabby Tabitha?" she chuckled.
"Yeah, I know, bit of a shit name"
"I'm sure it suits her perfectly"
"So, why theatre production?" I asked.
"Dunno. I guess I was always interested in plays and stuff, but not acting in them. I was more interested in the organisation side"
"I bet you've met some famous people"
"A few maybe"
"You're lucky, I don't get to meet any of them. We're kept hidden away in the dark corner"
She laughed "I'm sure I could arrange it. I can get you into rehearsals if you want"
"For *Macbeth*?"
"Yeah, they're starting next week"
"I'd like that"
"It's a date" she smiled, and finished her drink.
"Let me get you another" I said.
"You sure?"
"Yes, I'm sure" I smiled.
Was I sure though? It meant going inside. It was noisy and busy in there. I stood and ducked under the tree. Ok, let's do this.

I went inside, and joined the queue.
I could feel eyes on me, which at any other time would have made me run for the hills already.
However, not tonight. Tonight, I had something I had been lacking for years; courage.
I stood firm, and slowly got to the front of the line.
"Yes love?" The young barman asked.
"Two Aperol Spritz please"
"Coming right up" he smiled, and went off to make the drinks.
It took him a while to finish both of them, and then he returned.
"Two Aperol Spritz" he said, placing them on the bar.
"Anything else?"
"No thank you"
He tapped the till screen. "Eleven pounds forty please"
I tapped my card on the reader, and it went through.
"All done"
"Thank you" I picked up the drinks, and pushed my way awkwardly through the mass of people.
It was a relief to make it back out into the fresh air.
I ducked back under the tree carefully, so as not to spill the drinks.
"Thank you" Abigail said as I put the drink down in front of her. "How was that?"
"Terrifying" I smiled.
"You should have let me go"
"No, its fine. I need to get used to it" I said.
"You're doing really well" she said, placing her hand over mine. Again, the almost imperceptible spark of electricity surged through me.

We sat and chatted about her work, and the actors she had met.
Time seemed to fly by, because before I knew it, last orders were being called.
We'd had five Aperols already, and Abigail dashed in to get the last round.
My head felt like it was spinning.
Alternatively, was it the world around me?
I couldn't quite make it out. I took a few deep breaths, and got myself under control.
"I'm not sure that's a good idea" I said when she put the drinks on the table.
"Oh, shit. I forgot, you haven't had a drink for years! I'm so sorry. Here, I'll have both of them" she winked.
"Thanks" I smiled. "I'd best order a taxi" I pulled out my phone and booked a cab through the app.
"Fifteen minutes"
"Enough time for me to finish these" she smiled.
"What's the plan for tomorrow?" I asked.
"Laundry, cleaning, shopping. The usual Sunday routine. You?"
"Sleep most likely. Then a bit of work. May go out for a walk"
"Sounds perfect"
"Yeah, I guess"
"Oh, looks like your taxi is here" she said, looking down to the street below.
"Oh, I'd better go then" I said, standing. I rocked a little, but was otherwise fairly steady.
"I'll walk down with you, time for me to go home too I think"
"I can give you a lift" I offered.

"I live a minute or so away, you just get yourself home"
We walked down the narrow steps, and I walked over to the taxi.
"One minute please" I said. The guy nodded.
I turned and went back to Abigail.
"Thank you so much for inviting me out" I said.
"Thank you for coming. It was very brave"
"Happy birthday" I smiled.
"Thank y..."
Before she could finish, I leaned forward and kissed her. She stood and let it happen.
After, she stroked my hair, and said "You should go home, Taxi is waiting"
"I'm sorry" I said.
"Don't be" she smiled "Goodnight"
She turned, and walked off down the road.
What the hell had I just done?
Who had I become?
I got in the taxi and went home.

7. A Heart Void of Remorse.

I woke the following morning feeling like shit, and with a killer headache to match. Jesus. I was sure I'd only had like four or five drinks. How had I gotten back here? Ugh. This sucked. Now I remember part of the reason why I didn't drink; hangovers.
I dragged myself out of bed and walked to the fridge to get a bottle of water. For some reason, I checked the spare bedroom on the way. There was nobody there of course, I don't know why I had to check.
As far as I could remember, I'd had a great evening with Abigail. That was good. No painful memories.
I opened the fridge, took out a bottle of water, and drank greedily. I needed water. That would make the headache go away. But, I thought a couple of paracetamol would help it on its way faster. I popped two, and swallowed them down with a glug of water.
The cat rubbed against my leg, wanting food no doubt.
"Morning Tabby, you need food girl?"
The cat meowed, and I followed her to her empty bowl.
"Here you go" I said, filling it. I stroked her whilst she ate, then went and sat outside. I felt bad, but not sick at least. Water would help. Breakfast could wait.
I sat in a chair, and reclined it back.
Ugh. I hated hangovers. I was just ging to lay here until it passed. Or until the painkillers kicked in at least.

I woke a while later, feeling marginally better. I had slept for just over an hour.
My headache had been reduced to a marginally annoying background pain. I sighed with relief.
Tabby was on my lap, asleep.
"Hey, come on, I need to get up" I said, desperate for the loo.
She jumped down and I sprinted inside to empty my bladder.
I felt miles better after, and jumped in the shower. After carefully removing all the makeup from my face, I just stood under the hot water for a while. Wow. What a night. I'm sure it was pretty lightweight for most people, but not to a non-drinker. I wondered how Abigail was feeling. She was likely up and doing something wonderful. Whereas I was stood under the shower, trying to remember last night.
Oh shit.
Shit, shit, shit, shit, shit, shit.
I'd kissed her.
"Shit!" I shouted.
Oh my God. How was I going to face her? Shit. Shit. Shit.
But wait. Wait a minute. I checked my heartrate; 74.
If I was really worried, it would be over a hundred. Did that mean I wasn't really worried? Maybe I wasn't?
I mean, why should I be? It was just a kiss right?
Girls kissed their friends goodbye all the time.
Didn't they? It's what normal women did.
There was something missing... Remorse.
I felt zero remorse.

What the hell was happening to me? I should be on the floor, sobbing my eyes out with shame right now.
Yet here I stood. No tears, no racing heart, nothing.
I turned the shower off and wrapped myself in a towel. Something was wrong. I needed to see myself.
I rubbed the condensation from the mirror, and looked at my reflection. Same as yesterday.
I shook my head in disbelief, and went to the bedroom. I dried off and dressed. My dress had been casually discarded on the floor, so I picked it up and put it on a hanger. No stains. Perfect. I hung it on the wardrobe door and picked up my underwear. The underwear that had made me feel like superwoman. I smiled, and put it in the laundry basket. After towel drying my hair, I went to the kitchen to make some toast.
My phone. It was on the kitchen table.
I snatched it up and unlocked it; I had messages.
I opened WhatsApp and saw I had messages from my mum, James, and Abigail.
My heart stopped. Abigail. Shit. What if she was angry? What if she thought I was in love with her or something?
With a feeling of dread, I opened her message.

Hey, how's the head this morning?

That wasn't bad was it? I felt relief wash over me.
I smiled and typed: "Banging headache. I hate hangovers" I hit send.
Mum wanted to know how it had gone. Not sure what she was expecting. Though I did kiss her. Shit.

I refrained from telling her as such, and just said I had a great time.

James had a similar question, so I told him it was fine, no naked pillow fights.

That had always been something he mentioned when talking about girls. Naked pillow fights, feathers flying everywhere. Not sure where he'd gotten that idea from, porn most likely. I was pretty sure it didn't happen in the real world.

I put my phone down, and it buzzed immediately.

I picked it back up; Abigail.

Lol, yeah, bet you got a stonker. But you only had five drinks!

Ugh, now she must think I'm a lightweight. Still, better than her asking why I had kissed her.

I text back: "Yeah, bad times! Such a lightweight these days!"

She responded straight away: *Have a coffee and chill out.*

Still no mention of the kiss. Did she remember? Of course she did. Maybe she was waiting for me to raise it so as not to embarrass me.

I really didn't want to mention it, so just typed: "No regrets"

It was true. I had no regrets. No feelings of remorse (still). I felt quite happy about it really.

She text back: *None. Enjoy your day. X*

None? Did that mean she didn't regret me kissing her? I had no clue.

I text back: "And you. X"

No reply came, so I put the phone down, and ate my toast. I felt like I needed a walk. There was someone I could tell. Someone who wouldn't judge me.
At least, I hoped she wouldn't.

It was nice out, and the town was super busy.
Ugh, I couldn't wait for the summer to be over so I could walk the streets without bumping into thousands of tourists.
Headphones on, I made my way to the graveyard.
I picked a few flowers along the way, and placed them on her grave as I sat down.
"Morning Mary. Got you some flowers. Wow. I had quite the exciting night last night. Nothing *like that* mind, I just kissed someone. And you know what? I feel no remorse. Nothing. I actually feel fabulous"
No response came, of course. It never did. "Oh Mary, what am I to do? How do I face her? Yes, her. I know, shocking. Scandalous even. But, this is the twenty first century, you won't believe the things that are considered acceptable these days. You'd probably hate the modern world. Noisy, busy, dirty. I bet the air was far cleaner in your day"
I leaned back against her headstone "Were you married Mary? Your headstone has worn quite badly, so I can't really tell. If you were, I hope you were happy. I wonder if you have family out there now? If you do, I don't think they know you're here. Looks like I'm the only one that ever comes to see you. Still, never mind eh? At least we have each other"

I smiled, and opened my bag to check my phone. Shit. I'd left it at home.

"Looks like I left my phone at home Mary. Not that you'd know what a phone is. But, I'm sure you'd be amazed by it. Witchcraft!"

I smiled and got up.

"Gotta go. You have a nice Sunday, and I'll see you through the week sometime"

I patted her headstone and set off for home.

As I walked back, I got surrounded by a flock of white geese as I made my way through the RSC Gardens.

"Hey, I have no food" I protested. Was this a sign from Mary? Goose comms? Nah, that was nonsense.

I apologised again and walked on. They eventually gave up the chase and found another victim.

I found my phone where I'd left it; in the toilet. No messages. I wondered why I had returned home just to check. Was I *that* desperate?

Nah, surely not. Oh well, may as well watch the rest of *As You Like It*...

8. Nervous Anticipation.

I text Abigail a few times during the evening, but no response. The messages weren't even read. Shit.
Did that mean she'd remembered, and was angry?
Damn, I'd likely see her around work tomorrow.
Or would I? I didn't normally. Maybe I'd be able to just avoid her.
What? No. Cowards avoid people. No remorse, remember? If you see her, you see her. If you don't... you don't.
No biggie. Just go to work, and get on with your job.
Shit! My job! I needed to go through the Chinese curriculum! I ran into the hall and fumbled through my bag until I found the memory stick.
I flashed up my laptop, got a bottle of water from the fridge, and got to work.

I finally finished just after midnight. Jesus. I was exhausted, and my eyes hurt. I saved my notes, and went to bed. As I stood brushing my teeth, it came back to me; she hadn't read my messages. I finished, and ran to the bedroom to check my phone.
No messages, and she still hadn't read mine. Shit.
This was real; I was screwed.
I turned my phone off, and crawled into bed. This wasn't going to be a good night for me, I could feel it coming already.

I was right. I saw every hour of the night on the alarm clock.

If I had any sleep at all, it must have been a few minutes at most.

Thoughts of confronting Abigail haunted me all night. I was not looking forward to going to work. When the alarm finally sounded, I cried. My mind couldn't face it. I could just phone in sick, stay here all day.

Easily done. But so is getting up and going to work. I could clock a few hours to working from home so I could leave early. I had spent four hours reviewing the Chinese curriculum after all. That made me feel better. Slightly.

I got up and had a shower. It didn't do much to wake me up, but it felt good, nevertheless.

I dressed, had my usual breakfast, and went to work. The feeling of dread grew the closer I got to the iconic building.

What if she was waiting for me outside? Had she read my messages yet? I hadn't even checked my phone. Ugh. This was not a good start.

I locked up my bike and went straight in. No Marco's for me this morning. What if I saw her there?

I walked up the stairs to my office, and sat behind my desk.

Jenny came straight in, all fresh faced and enthusiastic.

"Wow, you look like crap. You ok boss?" she asked.

"Thanks" I smiled "I'm ok. Just didn't sleep is all"

"Oh, I see. Did you…"

I handed her the memory stick.

"Oh great, thanks" she said, clearly relieved "Any comments?"

"In a Word file on the drive"

"You're the best, thanks boss" she smiled, and went off to finalise the work.

She returned a ten minutes later and placed a cappuccino on my desk from the canteen.

"You're the best, Jenny" I smiled.

"You look like you could do with it" she smiled, and left me in peace.

I sipped the coffee. She was right; I did need it.

Why was I so nervous? I had been fine yesterday.

She hadn't read my messages. That's where this all stemmed from. Jesus. Was that all? I picked up my phone and checked. All the messages had blue ticks against them, indicating she'd seen them. Genius! No responses though, that wasn't good. Her status changed to online, and she started typing. Oh shit. Here we go.

But... Nothing. No message. She went offline, and that was it. That just made me feel ten times worse. I felt sick. Oh my God. She hated me.

I had messed up. It was over.

What? What was over? Nothing had started. I had kissed her, that was all. It wasn't like we'd slept together. Why was I so bloody worried all the time? What was wrong with me? I checked my heartrate: 97. Jesus. I did some deep breathing to bring it back down. Maybe my mother was right; maybe I did need to speak to someone. I supposed speaking to Mary didn't count; she had been dead for over two hundred years after all. Ugh.

I didn't want to speak to some stranger about my life. What good would it do? Make me better? Just like that? I doubted it. But yesterday had been so good.

That's why it hurt more. I had seen what better looked like.

I could feel tears welling up. This wasn't good.

The team would be busy for hours yet, so I was safe to just let go.

And I did. I sobbed loudly, letting all the emotion out.

And then, there was a knock at my door. The door opened; it was Abigail.

"Hey" she smiled.

But, her smile disappeared when she saw the tears.

"Oh shit, what's wrong?" she asked. She came in and closed the door.

"Hey, what's up?" She asked, putting her arm around me.

"I'm so sorry" I sobbed "I messed up"

"Because you kissed me?"

"Yes, and now you hate me" I said, still sobbing madly.

"What? I don't hate you"

"But you didn't reply" I said between sobs.

"Ah, yeah. Sorry. I fell asleep early yesterday, and didn't see your messages till I got to work. I was going to reply, but then got called into a meeting. After, I thought it better to come see you in person"

I banged my fist against my head "I hate my mind" I sobbed.

"Hey, don't do that. Look, Kate, everything is fine between us. I know you were a bit drunk, and the kiss meant nothing. I'm fine with it. Hey, look at me"

I looked up, and met her green eyes.

"I'm ok with it. Honestly. I was going to see if you maybe fancied lunch? We could go to see Mary if you like?"

"I'd like that"
Why did I feel like a small child? This was embarrassing.
Nobody was ever supposed to see me like this. Nobody.
Even my family hadn't seen me crash. Ugh, this wasn't good at all.
If she thought it funny, or odd, she didn't say. In fact, she didn't say anything; she just held me.
I had never felt the sensation of being held by anyone like this before. It felt safe.
My sobbing subsided after a while, and I wiped my eyes.
"God, I must look a right state" I said, wiping mascara from my cheeks.
"You look fine" she said "Don't worry about that. Are you ok?"
"No, not really. But, I'll manage" I said.
"You want me to go?"
"No. Please" I said, perhaps a little too quickly.
She smiled. "I have some time. Are you free for a coffee?"
I looked at the cup on my desk. I'd had a few sips, and it was probably cold by now.
"Sure" I said "That would be nice"
She opened her handbag and handed me a compact mirror "Here"
"Thanks" I smiled. I checked my face in the little mirror. Jesus. I opened a desk drawer and took out a pack of makeup wipes
"I'll need a minute" I said.
"I have an hour" she smiled "No rush"

I removed the makeup from my face, leaving nothing. Makeup free. Not that I used much anyway, but it felt weird.

"Ready" I said, handing back the mirror.

"Wow, you look amazing without makeup. You lucky sod"

"Swedish genes" I smiled.

"I hate you" she smiled, shaking her head "Come on"

9. Regrets can't Mend a Loss.

We walked down to the café, and ordered coffee. For once, there was a table free outside, so we took it.
"You sure you're ok?" she asked.
"I'm sorry you had to see that"
"Have you thought about talking to someone?"
"That's what my mother would say" I smiled. "But, yes, I have"
"Your mother sounds wise"
"My mother just wants to analyse me and rebuild"
"I'm sure she's just worried"
"You don't know my mother" I said "She's not really the affectionate, loving type"
"That's a shame. Can I ask how it happens? I mean, you told me earlier, but..."
"No, that's fine. I don't know. I can be happy one minute, then something trivial might happen to send me spiralling down out of control. It's a very dark place, and I'm not always strong enough to crawl out of it"
"Have you ever... You know..."
"Suicide? God no, never. I may be depressed, but I love life too much to do that"
"Thank God. Do you have medication?"
"I have some anti-anxiety tablets, that's about it. They work for me"
"But you didn't take them today?"
"I thought I'd be ok. I'd had two good days, you know? And I thought maybe, just maybe, I was getting a bit better"

"Maybe going out drinking was a mistake, sorry"
"No, really, I enjoyed it. I felt alive. Not because of the drinking, but you know, because I felt like a different person. I dressed nice and everything"
I leaned in closer "I wore nice underwear"
She giggled.
"I just felt good about myself"
"You looked amazing"
"So did you"
"Yeah, but I do that every time I go out. Sounds like it was a one-off for you"
"It has been a long time since I dressed up nice. I usually just wear this"
I was wearing trousers with a blue blouse. Not quite the scruffy image I usually portrayed.
"Well, ok, not this. This is work clothes. But you know what I mean"
"Baggy jeans and tees"
"Exactly"
"You don't want to draw attention to your figure"
"Is that what it is?" I asked. I hadn't really considered that before.
"You don't like people staring at you"
That explained my aversion to wearing athleisure clothing.
"Yes, I suppose so. I don't like being judged by my body"
"But your body is perfect, there's nothing to judge"
"Maybe that's the problem. People stare"
"Men"
"Yes"

"That's just nature Kate. Men look at women. Women look at men. Maybe not as obvious, but we do"
"How do you manage it?" I asked.
"What? Men looking at me? I just don't care because I know I'm not interested in any of them. It kind of helps. I'm not going to let anybody make me dress differently. However, I suspect it's not just about men ogling you. You just don't want to be seen by anyone"
"Are you sure you studied theatre production? Not psychology? You're very good at it"
"If psychology is about pointing out obvious facts, then yeah, I guess I'm good at it"
"You're right though"
"I know I am" she smiled "If nobody notices you, they can't interact with you. You're invisible"
"Exactly"
"Thing is though Kate, we all need someone in our lives. Even the strongest people"
"I had someone" I said.
"Sorry, I didn't mean to…"
"No, it's ok" I smiled. "My brother says the more I talk about Sean the better"
"He must have been quite the guy"
"You know how people say we all have a soulmate?"
"Yeah"
"He was my friend soulmate. We just connected and fitted together perfectly"
"Sounds like you were very lucky"
"I was. Until I let him go off on his own"
"Hey. That wasn't your fault"
"If I had been there…"
"You regret not going with him?"

"Of course"
"Does your regret change anything? Does it make you feel better to feel it?"
"Yes"
"You think *he* would want you to feel regret? You think he would be happy to see what it has done to you?"
"No"
"He would want you to find happiness"
"Yes. But it's difficult. We were always together, there for each other. We cried together, laughed together. I just felt like I could say or do anything around him. You know? There was never anything sexual, it was just the purest form of friendship"
Oh shit. I felt instantly bad. I had just described the perfect friendship, and we had only just become friends. What if she was upset? Or angry?
"That doesn't mean it was a one-off" I smiled "I'm starting to feel the same around you"
"That's a really nice thing to say"
"You make me want to be better, it's weird. I had two really good days. Because of you"
"I'm glad I'm able to make you feel that way" she smiled.
"And I'm probably just a drain on you. I don't want it to be like that"
"You're not a drain. Like I said, we all need someone"
Was there something else going on here? Something I wasn't seeing?
"Are you ok?" I asked.
She looked up, a look of surprise on her face "Why do you ask?"

"You've spent time fussing over me, but I've not even asked how you are. At all"
"Nobody does, its fine"
"Oh my God" I said "That's it"
"What?"
"People always ask me how I am because it's obvious there's something wrong with me. With you it's different"
"It is?"
"It is. You care so much about other people, but you are overlooked because people think your life is perfect. You're always so happy"
She stared at me with those bright green eyes. It felt like she was staring directly into my soul.
"I'm not always happy" she said "Nobody is always happy"
"Sorry, I didn't mean to pry" I said awkwardly. Had I struck a nerve? I felt bad.
"It's difficult to describe" she said "It's like wearing a mask sometimes"
"Ah. I know what you mean" I said "I call myself the she chameleon"
"The what?" she smiled.
"She chameleon. A chameleon changes colour to blend into the background. I do the same to disguise my moods. I'm always fine in work, because I have to be. If I go home to see mum and dad, I put on a different disguise. She chameleon"
"That's funny" she smiled "And a very clever analogy"
"Wish I could take the credit, but it's a song title"
"A song title?"
"My dad is a Marillion fan"

"Who?"

"Old-school band. Doesn't matter. It's the title of one of their songs. It stuck in my mind I guess"

"I like it. We're a pair of she chameleons"

My watch buzzed. "Shit, I have to go. I have a meeting with the Chinese"

"Sounds important"

"Could be. They have a lot of money, and they're not afraid to spend it on their kids' education"

"Good luck"

"Thanks"

"Meet you at twelve?"

"Perfect" I paused. "Thank you"

"Any time. See you later"

10. Cirrus Clouds Above.

I felt better after my chat with Abigail. Like a load had been lifted. She appeared to have a positive effect on my mood. Much like Sean. It helped me to prepare for my call with the Chinese, which went extremely well. They loved the curriculum, and had agreed to pay the hefty price we were asking. They did not even blink. I had just brought in a lot of money for the RSC, and I would make sure they remembered at my annual review.
I gave the team the afternoon off for doing such a great job, and they all disappeared off to the Dirty Duck to celebrate. They wanted me to join them, but I had another appointment to keep. And I had shopping to do before that.

I was a little early for my meeting with Abigail, purely by habitual force, so I sat on the steps people watching. I found people infinitely fascinating. I wondered what their stories were, what their lives were like. Did they have the same worries as me?
"People watching eh" Abigail said, sitting down next to me.
"Fascinating" I said.
"Agreed. I love it"
"Shall we?" I asked.
"Yeah, let's go"
We got up and walked along the Avon towards the Holy Trinity Church.

Without thinking, I took hold of her hand.
I'd seen normal women do the same, so why shouldn't we? She didn't react, and we walked on happily.
I picked a few flowers on the way, to replace the ones I'd brought yesterday.
"You bring her flowers?" Abigail asked.
"Yes, it seems apt"
"I guess it does. What do you know about this woman?" she asked as we sat next to the headstone.
"I can't even make out the name, it's so worn"
"I asked the church, and they checked their records"
"Makes sense"
"Mary Allen Brasher, Born 1752, died 1804"
"So young" she noted.
"People died young in those days. No medical miracle workers to keep them alive"
"Thank God for them now then. I couldn't imagine dying aged fifty two. Though, it seems miles off"
"I used to think thirty seemed miles off" I laughed.
"Speaking of which" I continued, opening my bag "I got you something. For your birthday"
"You didn't have to, fool" she said, but took the present anyway.
"Of course I did"
She unwrapped it slowly, and gasped. "Oh my God! Are you kidding? This is too much!"
"Ach, it's no bother"
"No bother? Coco Chanel?"
"You said you liked it" I shrugged.
"I *love* it, I could just never afford it"
"Well, now you don't have to" I smiled.

She leaned in and kissed me. Just a quick one, like friends often do, but a kiss, nevertheless.
"Thank you"
"No problem" I smiled.
She seemed happy, and that had been the idea. I wanted to make her happy.
We lay back on the grass and stared up at the sky.
"What beautiful clouds" she said "They look like feathers"
High above us, wispy, feather like clouds gazed down upon us.
"Cirrus clouds" I said.
"Cirrus?
"That's what they're called"
"You know about clouds?"
"I'm a dreamer"
She took hold of my hand, and we stared up at the clouds for a while. It was a beautiful moment.

After she had finished her lunch, it was sadly time to head back to work.
"What are you up to this afternoon?" she asked, spraying on some of her Coco Chanel.
My senses were momentarily tangled in the scent of her perfume. She smelled heavenly.
"You ok there?" she asked.
"Yes" I smiled. "Erm, nothing. I gave the team the rest of the day off, they're in the pub"
"You gave them the afternoon off? Wow, can I work for you?"
"We made a lot of money today, so I think they deserve it"

"You're a good person" she said.
"I try. What are you up to?"
"Auditions"
"You're involved in auditions?"
"Nah, I just get to watch"
"Sounds lovely"
"You should come"
"What?"
"Come along, it'll be fun"
"Oh, I don't know" I said. I don't know why I said that. There was nothing preventing me from going.
"Oh, if you're busy..." she said, slightly dejected.
"Of course I'm not. I'd love to come" I smiled.
Her face lit up, and her green eyes sparkled brightly in the afternoon sun.
"Great!"
She squeezed my hand a little as we walked. It made my heart skip a beat.

11. THE VIOLENT SILENCE.

Auditions were being held in the Swan Theatre, and we sat up in the first gallery, centre stage. The view was superb.
Down below us, actors, writers, directors, makeup people, and set designers milled about with purpose.
"Here he is" she said, squeezing my hand.
"Who?" I whispered.
"*Macbeth*"
A man walked out onto the stage and read a few verses from the play. His voice boomed around the theatre, pure, articulate, and masculine. He was great.
"He's perfect" I whispered.
"I know, isn't he just amazing?"
"Who is he?"
"Sam Heugen"
"I have no idea who that is, but he's pretty good"
She laughed "Yes he is"
We sat and watched more actors I hadn't heard of come and go. It was quite cool to watch though, regardless of that fact.
Abigail was fascinated by the whole thing, and was making notes about each of the actors that came and went. We didn't speak much, but just enjoyed each other's company instead. There was the occasional hand squeeze, but no words were spoken. I don't think words were needed. Even though we had only met a few days earlier. I felt good around her, I felt naturally at ease.

My watch buzzed, telling me I had a message.
I took my phone from my bag and checked. Mum. Would it be ok if she called? I text back: *Of course, still at work now though. Will let you know when I get home.*
"I have to go" I whispered "Mum wants to call, so I need to get home"
"Ok, no problem. Thanks for sitting with me, I really enjoyed it"
"Me too" I smiled "See you tomorrow?"
"No, I have to go down to London for a meeting"
"Oh, ok, no worries. I'll see you when you get back then"
"Yes you will"
I squeezed her hand gently, and quietly left the theatre.

I knew my mum just wanted to catch up on how things were going with Abigail. She never usually took so much interest in my life. We spoke maybe once or twice a month or so. I unlocked my bike and cycled home. The Cirrus clouds had disappeared, making the sky look like a deep blue empty canvas.
I put the bike in the garage and went inside. The cat came running up to me, desperate for food.
"I'm sorry Tabs, come on"
I fed the cat, and topped up her water.
Right. Mum.
I text her, to let her know I was home, and she called seconds later.
"Hi mum"
"Hello Kathrina, how are you?"

"Oh, I'm ok I suppose. Not much going on really"
"I see. How's work? Did you get the Chinese to sign?"
"Yes, they did so this morning"
"Oh, that's great news Kathrina. You don't sound overly happy about it though"
"Oh, I am" I said "I'm just tired. I barely slept at all last night"
"Oh, I see. Did Abigail stay over?"
"Mum!"
"What? Just asking"
"No, she didn't"
"Oh, ok. Well, it wouldn't have been a problem if she had would it?"
"Mother!"
"What?"
"I'm not gay, leave it alone"
"Oh, of course. How is your head?"
"Today? Not great. I broke down in work this morning, but was good for the rest of the day"
"What happened?"
"Paranoia happened. Anxiety happened. I didn't sleep all night out of worry"
"What were you so worried about? How did your date go?"
"It wasn't a date mum"
"Whatever you say dear. How did it go?"
"I told you already"
"Kathrina, you told me it was great. That was it. Just *great*"
"Well, there's not much more to say"
"Nothing? Did you just sit in silence all night?"
"What? Of course not"

"Well...?"
"Ugh. It was fine. We talked, had a few drinks, then I went home"
"And that was it?"
"Yes, what more do you want?"
"You sure that's it?"
"Yes"
"Kathrina..."
"Oh, ok, fine. I kissed her. There. Happy?"
There was silence.
"Hello?"
"You kissed her?" her voice sounded hopeful and happy.
"Yes"
"Did she kiss you back?"
"Mum!"
"What? Just curious"
"No. At least I don't think so. I can't really remember"
"And you were worried that she was maybe angry or somehow upset"
"Yes, of course"
"And was she?"
"No"
"So you worried for no reason"
"Mum, you know I can't help it"
She sighed "I wish you would talk to me Kathrina, I can teach you ways to cope with your anxiety"
"Mum, I'm fine"
"Doesn't sound like it. You broke down in work. Did anyone see?"
My turn to sigh "Abigail"
"And how did she react?"

"Like a loving, caring friend"
"My love, you know there's nothing wrong with being attracted to women right?"
"Mother!"
"There isn't. Your father and I both feel the same. We don't mind at all. As long as you're happy"
"Mum, I'm not gay"
"Has anything happened since you kissed her?"
"No"
"Kathrina…"
I sighed. "We held hands a lot"
"Oh, that's nice"
"And she kissed me"
"Oh!" she exclaimed.
"It was a thank you mum. I got her a birthday present"
"I see" she said, not convinced "What did you get her?"
"Coco Chanel"
"Kathrina!" she exclaimed "You bought her Chanel?"
"It's just perfume mum"
"It's more than that, and you know it"
"She said she liked it when I wore it on Saturday night"
"You wore Chanel?"
"It just smells nice mum"
"Of course dear"
"Have you finished analysing me now?"
"What? We're just chatting"
"Mum, we never *just chat*"
"You're terribly suspicious Kathrina. I just want to know about my daughter's life. Is that too much to ask for?"
"Mum, you've never been interested in my life"

Silence. Shit.
"I'm sorry. I shouldn't have said that"
"That hurt Kathrina"
"I'm sorry"
"I've always been here for you"
"Where were you when Sean died?" I asked evenly.
"I was there for you!" she exclaimed.
"No you weren't"
"I was, I came to see you, I asked how you were"
"I didn't need a bloody psychologist!" I shouted "I needed my mother. I needed you to take me in your arms and tell me everything was going to be alright. I needed love, not analysis"
Silence.
I knew she was hurting. I knew I'd overstepped a line. But I didn't care. It needed to be said at some point. She needed to hear the truth. I could feel my heart racing like mad. I needed to calm down.
"I'm sorry mum, but I needed to say that"
Silence.
"I do love you" she said eventually.
"I know you do mum. In your own way. You're just not great at showing it"
"I'm sorry" she said quietly.
"I love you too mum. I haven't always been the best daughter for you, I know that"
"Don't say that" she said. I could hear her welling up.
"You're perfect"
"Nobody is perfect mum"
"You're my perfect little girl" she cried "I miss you so much"
"Why haven't you ever told me that before?"

"I don't know. I just... I just can't. I'm not good at this kind of stuff"
"Mum, I'm your daughter, you should be able to tell me you love me"
"I know"
"Just occasionally. You don't even have to say it, you can message me"
"I love you. I'm so very proud of you. You've achieved so much, and endured such sadness. I just want you to get better"
"So do I mum, but there's no magic wand"
"I know. I just want to help"
"I don't want you to help me like that mum. Just be there for me. That's all I need. I don't want to be analysed by my own mother"
"Ok, fair enough"
"I'm sorry for what I said, it was cruel" I said.
"It was the truth. I'm proud that you were able to tell me"
"I also lied to you"
"How so?"
"I do like Abigail, I think she's beautiful, warm, loving, caring, intelligent, witty. All that good stuff"
"Give it a chance"
"I will. I promise"
"Good"
"Bye mum"
"By Kathrina. Love you"
"Love you too mum"

I hung up and put my phone down. Jesus christ. I had just shouted at my mother.

Regardless of whether she deserved it or not; it had been uncalled for. I felt like dirt.

I sat for a long while, just staring into space. The house was quiet. Deadly quiet. I could feel the angry silence closing in on me, like a black cloak enveloping my very being.

This was not going to happen. Not today.

I got up, and went out for a walk.

12. Hold Me Like You Mean It.

I walked towards the river, not really knowing where I was going. I just needed to get away from the silence. It was almost seven o'clock, and the tourists had thinned out a bit. There were still plenty of people about, but not the ant-like masses there were during the day. I sat on a bench by the riverbank, watching the row boats glide past. They tried their hardest to practice without hitting any of the swans or geese, of which there were dozens.
Working on instinct, I pulled my phone out and text Abigail: I need to see you.
She text back almost immediately.
Are you ok?
I need you to hold me.
Where are you?
On a bench, next to the rowing club.
I'll be there in five. Don't move.
I'll be here.

I put my phone down and stared out at the water for a while. Geese and swans glided past, hoping I had some food to give them. I didn't. I never did. But they still always came, full of hope. A bit like me, I supposed.
"Hey, there you are, what's wrong?" Abigail said, arriving a little out of breath. She sat next to me.
"I need to be held" I said.
"Of course, come here" She held out her arms, and I fell into her bosom.

She held me tight. It was exactly what I needed.
I was home.
She stroked my hair, and kissed my head.
"What happened?"
"I shouted at my mum" I said.
"Why?"
"She was asking loads of questions about our night out, and I told her off. I said she had never been interested in my life"
"Ouch. How did she take that?"
"Badly, obviously. She said she had always been there for me. I asked her where she was when Sean died, and she told me she had been there"
"Had she?"
"Yes, but not as a mum. I shouted at her, I said that I didn't need a psychologist, I needed my mother. To hold me and tell me it was going to be ok"
"Wow. What did she say?"
"She asked why I hadn't said that before. And that she was proud of me, of what I had achieved. All that kind of stuff"
"That's good isn't it?"
"Yes, it is. I also told her I lied to her"
"About what?"
I paused. "About you"
"About me? What about me?"
"I told her I wasn't interested in a relationship with you, and insisted I wasn't gay"
"That was a lie?" she asked, voice full of hope.
"Yes. I like you. I like you a lot. I feel good around you. My mind is good around you. I want you in my life. Sod it. I *need* you in my life"

"Wow" she said.
Wow? Wow?? Was that it?
I let her go and sat up.
"Just wow? Is that all you.." But I didn't get a chance to finish. Her lips were on mine, and her arms around me, pulling me closer. I had never felt that good in all my life. That moment, that exact moment? Would be with me forever.
When she finally pulled away, I was left completely breathless.
"Ok" she said, brushing her hair back over her ears.
"Ok?"
She nodded "Ok. But I need to know one thing"
"What?"
"I need you to be one hundred percent invested"
"That sounds very clinical"
"You know what I mean Kate"
"I do. Look, we barely know each other. Maybe we should take it slow, and get to know each other better first"
"Ok, how do we do that?" she asked.
"We date"
"Date?"
"Yes, we go on dates. You may not like me after going out with me a few times"
"Or you me"
"So let's keep it casual. We'll go on dates, nothing heavy"
She thought for a moment, then said "Fine"
"Just fine?"
"You're right. We shouldn't rush into anything. Let's date. No mention of the dreaded L word"

"Fantastic We can use fond instead of…" I said, and held her hand.
"Works for me. You like holding hands" she smiled.
"Yes, it's very intimate"
"I like it too"
I squeezed her hand "Thank you"
"For what?"
"For coming, it means a lot"
"You needed me"
"Yes"
"I'm here for you. Only you"
"As am I"
"You going to be ok?"
I nodded and smiled. "Yeah, I am"
"Good"
"You should go, it's getting late"
"Yeah, it is. You should get home too"
"I should"
Awkwardly, we stood and hugged.
"Take care of yourself" she said.
"Thank you, I will. See you tomorrow?"
"Count on it" she smiled.
We separated, and walked away in our respective homeward directions.
"Hey!" she shouted from behind me.
I turned "What?"
"My girlfriends call me Abi"
I laughed "Goodnight Abi"
"Goodnight Kate"
We turned, and walked home.
I had this enormous feeling of extreme joy in my chest, like I had just been reborn.

13. Darkness Know Not My Heart!

I felt like I was walking on clouds on my way home. Had that really just happened? I had a girlfriend? Me? But I wasn't gay. Was I? I didn't really know what I was. But, that was neither here nor there. All that mattered was that I felt happy. Like all the darkness had been sucked out of my heart.

I got home and hugged the cat who was sitting on the doorstep. "Oh Tabitha, isn't the world just wonderful?" Whether or not the cat agreed is debatable, but she purred, nevertheless.

We went inside and I danced around the living room. I was happy. Jesus. I couldn't remember the last time I'd been this happy. I put some music on and got my clothes ready for work. Gone were the trousers and blouse. Tomorrow, I would wear a dress.

After choosing the red dress, I lay back on the bed and bought some new underwear. Nice underwear. Sexy underwear. No more boring cotton for me. Though, I may just keep them in case I have a bad day. I wanted to look good for Abi. I wanted to look and feel good for myself. I was sick of being beaten down by my own insecurities. I supposed I had to speak to my mother. No, I *wanted* to speak to my mother. Jesus, I'd never actually *wanted* to speak to her.

I picked up my phone and dialled.

"Kathrina? Everything ok?" She sounded concerned.

"Mum, I'm so happy" I said, sounding all giddy.

"Are you drunk?"

"What? No mum. I just saw Abi"
"Abi? Not Abigail?"
"She said I should call her Abi seeing as she was now my girlfriend" I said, and waited for her response with crippling anticipation.
"Oh my God Kathrina!" she said "Are you serious?" She sounded stupendously happy.
"Yes mum, we're going to go on dates and everything"
"Oh my girl, I'm so happy for you" She sounded like she was going to cry again. "That's the best news ever"
"I know" I said excitedly.
"I'm going to go tell your father, he'll be made up"
"Ok mum, speak soon?"
"Yes, we will. I love you Kathrina"
"I love you too mum"
I threw the phone down and went over to the mirror. My hair. Ugh. It was so short. Oh well, it would have to do. Though, I was going to let it grow again. I wanted to be a woman. A vivacious, happy woman.
"Small steps Kathrina" I reminded myself. "Small steps"
I took a deep breath, and went for a shower.
After, I sat and moisturised, then put my pyjama's on. It was only nine o'clock, but I was tired.
I fed and watered the cat, then went to bed.

I woke the following morning before the alarm went off. Normal routine resumed! I felt happy, fresh, and ready for the day.
I had a quick shower, dried my hair, had breakfast, got dressed, did makeup, fed cat, and left for work.
The bike would have to stay home today, I couldn't ride it wearing a dress.

I shrugged, and walked to work.

It was a lovely morning, and I had the feeling it was going to be a good day.

I didn't even care about the people watching me as I walked. Sod them. They weren't going to drag me down.

I walked past the RSC and continued on to get coffee from Marco.

"Mama mia!" he said as I walked in.

He came out from behind the counter to get a better look.

"Signora Kate! You look beautiful! Oh!" he said, clutching his chest.

"Morning Marco" I said, smiling shyly.

"You have a boyfriend?" he asked, pretending to be hurt.

"Girlfriend Marco"

"Oh! You break my heart signora Kate" he said. in his broken English.

"Can I get a coffee please?"

"Of course" he smiled "I make it now. You sit"

I sat at a table and waited.

He came over a few moments later with my coffee.

"This is the lovely signora you brought in?"

"Yes, she's called Abigail"

"She is lovely" he smiled "You look happy"

"Thank you. I am"

"Is good. Here, I give you two cannoli now. You cost me!" he said theatrically.

I kissed his cheek "Thank you Marco"

"Oh, mama mia!" he smiled, acting heartbroken.

"See you tomorrow" I said.
"Ciao bella"
I walked to the RSC with a spring in my step, and love in my heart. Love? Not that I thought I loved Abi, it was far too early for that. Just love in general. We'd agreed to stick with being fond of each other for the time being, and that was fine by me. I was extremely fond of her.
I drew some admiring looks as I walked through the building up to my office.
"Wow" Jenny said as I walked in "Special occasion?"
"Nope. Just feeling happy" I said.
"Well, God bless you Kate" she smiled "You look lovely"
"Thank you Jenny" I smiled "What's on the agenda today?"

After spending the morning going through the design for the new website, which was due to launch in September, I had a call from Catherine O'Neill, my manager.
"Morning Kate"
"Morning Catherine"
"Kate, have you got five minutes? I'd like to have a word"
"Oh, yes, sure. Now?"
"If convenient?"
"Of course, I'll be right up"
"Great"
She hung up.
What does she want? Is this because I gave the team the afternoon off? Shit.

I knew I should have checked with her first. Ok, relax. I took a breath, and walked up to her office.

The door was open, so I knocked on the doorframe.

"Kate" she smiled "Come in"

I went in and sat in the chair opposite her.

"Is this about yesterday?" I asked nervously "I know I should have checked with you first, sorry"

"What? No. You're free to make decisions about your own team Kate" she smiled.

"Oh, ok"

"Change of image?" She asked.

"Bit more girly" I said "Thought I'd try it out"

"And?"

"I like it"

"I suits you"

"Thank you"

"Kate, I wanted to talk to you about your contract"

"My contract?"

"Yes, you're on a fixed term contract, due to expire October first"

Shit. I'd forgotten about that.

"Ah, yes" I said "I'd forgotten"

"You did good work with the Chinese, Kate. Really good work. I'm to pass on a heartfelt thanks from the very top. And my own, of course"

"Oh, thank you. The team did all the work really"

"Under your leadership and direction"

"I suppose"

"You did good Kate. You made us a lot of money. A *lot* of money"

"Thank you"

"As a token of our appreciation, I have been authorised to make your position a permanent one"
"Permanent?"
"As in no end date. We want you to run the Curriculum department indefinitely. In fact they're pretty desperate to keep you"
"Oh, that's amazing news, thank you"
"You'll get a pay rise, and a one-off bonus as an extra thank you"
"A bonus?"
"Kate, you have any idea how much money you brought in with that contract? It was all your idea"
"I suppose"
"Look, the bonus isn't much, two thousand, after tax. I fought for more, but they wanted to increase your salary instead"
"Two thousand? Wow. That's more than enough"
"Are you sure? I tried to get more"
"No, really, I am very grateful"
"Excellent" she smiled "Your new contract will be sent to you for approval sometime today, you'll need to read it and sign if you're happy"
"I will"
She stood and held out her hand. I stood and shook it
"Thank you Kate. And I'm really glad we're keeping you, you've more than deserved it"
"So am I" I smiled.
"Just for future reference; you don't need to check with me for team decisions"
I nodded "Noted"

I walked back to my office with a giddy spring in my step. I had completely forgotten about my contract. But, now I was permanent! Moreover, I had a two grand bonus! That would pay for my flights to see my brother for Christmas this year. I walked straight down stairs, and out to Anna's Bakery to get cakes for the team.

14. The Air You Breathe.

I spent the hour after lunch going through my new contract. It was identical to my current one, except for the duration, which was permanent, and the salary, which had gone from 38 to 43K a year. Five grand pay rise! I signed it digitally, and sent it back to HR. I was now officially the RSC Curriculum Department Manager. Me! I was so chuffed.
Just then, my phone buzzed. I picked it up and saw I had four messages from Abi.
Morning!
You want to do lunch?
You ok?
Are you ok?

Shit. I text back immediately: Sorry, hectic day, was in with my manager.
Coffee? You can tell me all about it.
Sure, meet downstairs in five.

I went downstairs, and met her in reception.
"Oh wow, look at you" she smiled, "You look fantastic"
"Thanks, you look fantastic yourself"
Her long brown hair was in two plaits, she was wearing a long brown skirt, and a lovely white blouse.
"You smell nice" I winked.
"Oh this? Just some cheap rubbish I got for my birthday"
"Cheeky"

"Come on, let's get coffee" she smiled.
We held hands as we walked out to the terrace café. There were a few tables free, so we sat down at one.
"I'll get these" I said "What can I get you?"
"Decaff Latte?" she said.
"Sure"
I went up and ordered the drinks. I looked back and saw her sitting in the sun. She looked beautiful. I was so incredibly lucky.
"All done" a voice said behind me. I had been so transfixed that I hardly heard him.
"Oh, thank you"
I took the drinks back to our table and sat down.
As I did so, I could smell the heavenly scent of Chanel. Beautiful.
"So, what's with the boss?" she asked.
"Oh, yeah. So, I have a contract that expires in October"
"You're leaving?" she asked, looking worried.
"No, they offered me a permanent position, and a pay rise, and a bonus"
"Wow!" she said, sitting back in her chair "Get you!"
"The Chinese contract sealed it for them apparently"
"Good for you" she smiled "That's amazing news"
"Thanks"
"What are you going to spend your bonus on?"
"You"
"Me? Don't be daft"
"I want you to come to America with me for Christmas"
"What? Oh, I don't know Kate"
"You don't want to?" I asked, worried.

"Are you kidding? Of course I do. But, it's your money; you should spend it on yourself"
"In a way, I am. My brother has a new girlfriend, and he has asked me to go over to spend Christmas with them. I'd be the third wheel without you"
"Are you sure?"
"Of course"
"Ok then" she beamed "I'd love to!"
"Oh, you've made my day" I said, relieved "I was worried you'd say no"
"Why would I say no to a free holiday?"
"I don't know, I thought maybe you'd think it was too soon"
"Don't be daft. I want to spend time with you"
"And I with you" I said, inhaling the intoxicating scent of her perfume.
"So..." she said "There's a party at my house tomorrow night"
"A party?" Alarm!
"You know, people, drink, food, chatter. That kind of thing"
"I don't know Abi..."
"For me?"
I sighed "Ok. Just for you"
"Genius" she said, clapping her hands in excitement. "Do I need to bring anything?"
"Just bring a bottle of wine, nothing too fancy mind"
"I can do that" I lied; it would be fancy.
"Look. I've been reading up on anxiety and stuff. And I just wanted to say something to you"
She took hold of my hands and looked deep into my eyes.

"You *are* good enough for me. If anything, you are *too* good for me. I don't want you ever thinking otherwise, ok?"

A tear rolled down my cheek.

"Hey, no need to cry. I just wanted you to know that, so you don't have to sit at home worrying about it"

"Thank you. That means a lot"

At that very moment, I knew; I loved her. I worshipped the very air she breathed. She was perfect. Fondness be damned!

I went up to the toilets and fixed my makeup. It wasn't too bad this time, just a bit of mascara required.

I had thought of the America trip on the spur of the moment, and thought it would be a great idea. Maybe I should have discussed it with her first. Didn't really matter now. All that mattered was that she was coming with me. And that made me happy.

The rest of the day was spent going through the website design, and drawing up lists of plays I needed to watch in order to get the curriculum updated.

The entire curriculum was aimed at secondary school level kids, trying to get them more interested in Shakespeare. It was an exciting project, and I was honoured to be involved in it.

I walked home after work, enjoying the late afternoon sunlight. The swans and geese swam over as I walked towards the bridge, hoping for a feed. Maybe I should just get some for them. Nothing like a bit of peer pressure!

As usual, given the space to do so, my mind started working overtime, and doubts crept in.
I was worried about going to this party at Abi's place, not to the point that it would keep me awake all night, but still worried. I hadn't been to a party for ages.
The thought of her being there made it better, as I knew she would look after me. It was a bit sad that I needed looking after at all, but hey; such is life.
I got home and made a cup of tea, then grabbed my laptop and went out into the back garden. I had shopping to do. Dresses weren't going to buy themselves.
I spent a good hour or so browsing and buying. By the time I'd finished, I'd bought five dresses and more sandals to go with them.
I also got some new nail varnish, more neutral colours, the old black stuff was already in the bin.
Who was I becoming? Hopefully someone Abi would stay interested in. I wanted to look good for her, not like some scruffy tom-boy.
The doorbell rang, so I went out to see who it was. Although I already knew; delivery.
The delivery man had a few packages for me, which I took into the bedroom. I knew exactly what was in them; my new underwear.
Excitedly, I unwrapped it all, and spent an hour or so sorting out my top drawer. The cotton stuff was banished to the bottom drawer; time for the sexy stuff.
Once that was done, I took the rubbish out to the recycle bin and text my brother, asking if I could bring a friend for Christmas.

He text back half hour or so later saying it was fine, and he was looking forward to my meeting Jane.

How's that going?
Cat, she's lovely, I totally adore her
Well, that's good, isn't it?
Yes, it is. I'm really happy. Speaking of which, how are you?
Oh, I'm ok. Got my contract made permanent today.
Hey, that's great news!
Yeah, I'd completely forgotten about it
Any other news?
Not really
Sure?
Ah. You've spoken to mum
Yes…
That woman, I swear to God…
Hey, it's not her fault, she's just happy for you
That's good, because I shouted at her on the phone
Yes, she mentioned that. Bit awkward
Oh God, is she still angry?
The opposite; she couldn't be happier
Wow
So?
We're an item
Ha! I knew it!
What?
You're a lezzer!
You're a dick
Sorry. Anyway, how are things going?
Things are going slow, which is what we both want

Good. As long as you're happy. I assume she's coming for Christmas?
If that's ok?
Of course it is, I can't wait! Hey, I've got to get back to work, stay happy!
You too

Great. So, now my brother would eternally refer to me as "Lezzer". Genius. I smiled. It *was* kind of funny. Funny. This whole situation was funny. I only hoped that Abi realised what she was taking on.
Wait.
A thought came to me.
I went to my home office, rummaged through the drawers, and found what I had been looking for.
I checked the ink level in my fountain pen, and started writing.

I had expected to be awake for most of the night, worrying about this bloody party. But, I hadn't. I slept rather well actually.
Still woke before the alarm though. I looked around at my sterile living environment and wondered what it would be like to have someone else here. Would they make a mess? Was she messy? I had no idea. I mean, everyone is messy compared to me. I hoped she wasn't. However, being messy is what normal women do. I would just have to learn to accept it. Or at the very least, live with it.
Anyway, no time to laze about; time to get up.

15. THE ART OF SOLITUDE.

I put the card in my bag, and walked to work. This wasn't going to be easy. I text Abi on the way, asking if she'd be free for a tea or coffee sometime today.
Her response came through as I was walking through the front doors of the RSC. I showed my pass, and walked upstairs to read it in my office.
I threw my bag down, and sat on the desk.
Yeah sure. I'm free at ten for a while if that's ok?
Perfect, see you then.

Two and a half hours to go. You'll be fine.
I flashed up my laptop and went through my emails.
Email from HR acknowledging receipt of my contract and congratulating me.
The rest was official RSC stuff, and one from Jenny with a summary of progress to date on the website. The web designers had been busy; they'd have a few samples ready for me to view by the end of next week. Excellent.
My phone buzzed. I picked it up.
Dad. He never called. Something was wrong.
I answered immediately.
"Dad? Everything ok?"
"Morning my angel, yes, everything is fine. I just wanted to speak to you is all. It's been a while"
"It has. How are you?
"Me? Oh, you know, busy as always. I have a big court case coming up, you'll see it in the papers no doubt"

"Nobody my age reads newspapers dad"
"Ugh, ok, you'll see it online then"
"Better" I chuckled.
"You sound happy"
"I am happy"
"That's good to hear Cat"
My God, he hadn't called me Cat since I was like ten or something.
"Thanks dad"
"I'm genuinely pleased for you Cat, you found love. That's never easy"
"Love? I wouldn't go that far" I said. Well, actually, it was love wasn't it? What else could it be?
"Early days, I get it" he said, saving me.
"Yes, it is. I have other news"
"Oh?"
"My position got made permanent, I'll be in charge of the Shakespeare Curriculum for the UK and Overseas"
"My God, that's great news angel, well done. Is that because of the Chinese deal? I assume it went well?"
"More than well. I brought in a tonne of money"
"That's my girl" he said "Well done"
"And I got a pay rise. Oh, and a bonus"
"A bonus? Well, you can take me for dinner sometime then"
"I'm using it to take Abi to Seattle for Christmas"
"You're not home for Christmas?" he asked, slightly taken aback.
"Your sons' idea dad. He invited me"
He laughed "Don't you worry about us Cat, we'll probably go skiing somewhere if you're not here"
I laughed. "Oh I see, like that is it? Charming"

"What's good enough for the goose…"
"Yeah, yeah, ok. Don't rub it in"
"Did James tell you about Jane?"
"He mentioned her briefly, early days there too"
"Yeah, but he seems happy"
"Both my kids are happy. What more could a father ask for?"
"You know he called me a lezzer?"
He laughed. "Really?"
"Yeah"
"And, you mind?"
"No, of course not. I know he's just being an idiot"
"Sounds about right. Oh, gotta go angel, I'm being summoned"
"Good talking to you dad, love you"
"Love you too Cat"

I hadn't heard my father's voice for some time. I missed him. He had always been there for me, unlike mum.
He was the first person to call me after Sean had died. I would always love him for that.
Right, I felt better about my meeting with Abi now. Thanks dad.
I spent the rest of the time watching *Macbeth*, making notes, and just falling in love with the words. I really wanted to go and see the new production, but it was sold out.
My watch buzzed; reminder for my meeting with Abi.
I closed the laptop and picked up my bag. My heartrate increased instantly. Relax, you got this remember?

I walked down to the lobby with a mind full of doubts and millions of reasons not to give her the card. No. I needed to do this.

I took a breath, and walked out into the sunshine.

"Kate! Over here!" Abi waved from a table on the terrace. She had already got the coffees in. What a woman.

I walked over and kissed her cheek "Morning"

"Morning, you ok?"

"Yeah, I just spoke to my dad"

"Was he ok with everything?"

"Over the moon"

"That's good then isn't it? You look worried"

"Listen Abi, I need to say something. You said yesterday that you'd been reading up on anxiety, and told me I was good enough for you. I really appreciate that, it was lovely"

"But…"

"No but. I have something for you. You can read it now, or read it later. I don't mind either way. It's just something that I wanted to tell you, explain, you know, what my head is like. What it's like being me"

I handed her the card.

"Can I read it now?"

"Of course" I said, slightly uneasy, looking around.

"You sure? I don't want to make you feel uncomfortable"

"No, it's fine. Please read it"

She opened the envelope and took out the card. It had a picture of Hamlet on it. I'd gotten it cheap in the RSC shop a while back.

"Hamlet eh?" she said.

I smiled nervously.
She opened it and started reading.

My dearest Abigail.

I wanted to try express to you in words how my mind works, how I am. It's important to me that you understand, if we are to go forward together.
I didn't really know how else to tell you this, but these words just spilled out:

I could feel alone
In a cast of thousands
I could feel alone
Even in your arms

I could feel alone
With a love so true
I could feel alone
Surrounded by you

Loneliness is real
Loneliness is true
Loneliness exists
When I'm with you

I feel alone
Even when I'm not
I feel alone
Like it's all I've got

Loneliness is pain
Loneliness is dread
Loneliness destroys
Leaving me for dead

I could feel alone
In a sea of friends
I could feel alone
When the music ends

They say the loneliest number is One,
But that's not always true
It's possible to be alone,
Even when there are Two

Kate. X

I could see tears forming in her eyes as she read. Were they good tears or bad tears? I couldn't tell. She read it again, and again. By the time she put it down, the tears were rolling down her beautiful cheeks.
"I'm sorry" I said "I didn't mean to upset you"
"Upset me? Kate, this is beautiful. You wrote this?"
"Yes"
She reached over and kissed me.
"That's the most heart-warming text I've ever read"
"Thank you. Does it make sense?"
"Perfectly so" She took out a tissue and wiped her eyes.
"God, now it's my turn to ruin my makeup" she laughed.
"Sorry, I didn't mean to…"

"Kate, you don't need to apologise to me. Not for this" she held up the card "Never"
"I wasn't sure how you'd react to be honest. I've been shitting it all morning"
She laughed "I can't imagine anyone taking this the wrong way. It's beautifully written"
"I guess anxiety is an endless sea of inspiration" I said.
"Must be. I will treasure it forever"
I blushed.
"Are you sure you want to come tonight? It's perfectly fine if you don't"
The party. Shit. I'd forgotten about that.
"Of course I'll come. I can't promise to stay all night though"
She took hold of my hands.
"You go whenever you feel you need to. I understand"
"Thanks. In lighter news, I spoke to my brother, he's more than happy for you to come"
"That's good" she smiled "I can't wait"
"He called me a lezzer"
"The cheeky bastard!" she laughed.
"I know right?" I giggled.
"I'll have some choice words for him when I see him" she joked.
We laughed and finished our coffee.
"Thank you for this" she said, holding up the envelope.
I nodded.
"One thing?"
"What?" I asked.
"If it ever gets this bad" she said, still holding up the envelope "You let me know immediately. No matter what"

"I promise"
"You'd better" she smiled.

I walked back to the office greatly relieved. I had written the card out in one go. The words had just spilled from my pen. I had been extremely anxious about her reaction. I shouldn't have been, of course, but I just couldn't help it. Now though, I was feeling good about myself again. Being around Abi made me better. She was like a drug.
But one I wasn't ashamed to be addicted to.

16. Dancing Shadows.

You'll be fine.
That was what Abi had been texting me all day. Would I be fine though? In a flat full of noise and people? There'd be drinking and dancing going on. I was definitely not going to be dancing. There would be no dancing. Nuh-uh.
Drinking though? Maybe. But not too much. I'll want to keep a clear head so I don't end up doing something I regret.
Though... I had kissed Abi after a few drinks, and look where that had gotten me. In a relationship.
I hadn't seen Abi all day, as she'd been really, really busy with the new production. I'd been pretty busy myself to be honest, I'd been going over the content for our *The Winter's Tale* section of the website.
Going through the material reminded me that I needed to read or watch the production so I could update my notes.
I checked my watch; almost home time.
Time had gone pretty quickly today, meaning the party was drawing ever closer to reality.
"Hey Kate, you got a minute?"
Jenny was stood in the doorway, with a concerned look on her face.
"Of course, come in" I smiled.
She came in and sat opposite me.
"What's up? You don't look too good" I said.
"It's my mum, she's not well"

"Oh no, what's wrong?"
"Well, they don't really know yet. She was taken to hospital last night"
"Why are you still here?" I asked.
"Oh, I didn't want to just run off, I know how busy we are"
"Jenny, go home"
"Are you sure?"
"Of course, go home. Be with your mother"
"Thanks Kate" she smiled "I really appreciate it"
"Family comes first Jenny, it's never a problem. I'm sure we'll manage for however long you need"
"Thanks, I'll make it up to you"
"No need, go see your mother. I hope she's alright. Let me know" I said.
She thanked me again, and left.
Wow. I thought of my own mum, and what I would do if she was ill. Would I be able to just go down to see her? Leave the team behind? Would I actually want to go see her? Of course I would. Don't be stupid.
I'd need to speak to Catherine about promoting Jenny so she could lead the team if I was ever out.
Ok, time to go home. I sighed loudly and packed up my laptop.

The walk home was pleasant; the weather was nice, and there weren't many people around. Not that I noticed much of it, I was too preoccupied with my anxiety about the party.
I checked my phone, and had three messages from Abi, making sure I was still coming. I text back that I'd be there. Seven o'clock, as agreed.

Her reassurances meant a lot to me, they gave me the confidence I otherwise lacked.

I fed the cat and threw my bag on the bed. Some parcels had arrived, so I opened them.

Ah, my new dresses.

I picked a nice yellow one, and a matt yellow nail varnish. I had some white trainers to go with it; hopefully Abi wouldn't spill her drink all over these ones.

I had a shower and did my legs. Oh, how I envied men! They could just shower, dress, and go out. We had a lot more to think about before we could leave the house. I supposed it was all pressure of our own making. After drying off, I moisturised and sat at my little makeup table. My hair was so short! Ugh. I regretted having it cut so much! Mum had told me I would, and she had been right. I did what I could with it, and got dressed. I had bought a nice bra and pants set which was white with daisies on it. It went perfectly with the yellow dress. I sat in my underwear and did my nails. I watched a bit of TV whilst they dried, and the cat came in to keep me company. She sat on the end of the bed, and curled up into a ball.

"Lucky you! You get to sleep. I have to go to a party. You know what a party is Tabby? Noisy, horrible, with lots of loud humans!"

The cat said nothing; she just closed her eyes and went to sleep.

When my nails were dry, I put on my dress and shoes. I checked myself in the mirror; lovely. I didn't want to over-do the makeup, so I just did my eyelashes, and put a bit of lippy on.

I sprayed on some Chanel, and was ready. Ready to go.
To the party.
Dread hit me instantly.
I opened my handbag and took a pill from the strip I kept in there for emergencies. It would help. I wish I didn't have to take them, but what choice did I have?
I really didn't want to be a nervous wreck. Not tonight. Not for Abi.
I took a picture of myself and sent it to mum.
I knew she'd appreciate it. And she did. She text back straight away, telling me how beautiful I looked.
She didn't add "If only you hadn't cut all your hair off", but I knew she was thinking it.
Satisfied, I picked up the bottle of Italian rosé I had bought from Marco this morning, and went out.
Out to the party.

I decided to walk to Abi's flat, as it wasn't really that far. Besides that, it was a lovely evening. It had cooled somewhat, enough to make it pleasant. I got some admiring looks as I walked, but I ignored them.
Last thing I wanted to do was interact with people.
I just wanted to get there, and get this over with.
When I got to the address she'd given me, I stood by the front door for a moment, staring at the doorbell.
Ringing it would take me inside. And inside was noisy.
I could hear it from the street. Manic Street Preachers were playing, and loud conversation accompanied them. I liked the Manics, which made it slightly less horrible. I had expected loud dance music. I hated loud dance music. That's a positive, right?
Time to go in, she'll be wondering where you are.

I raised my arm slowly, and pushed the bell.

A few seconds later, the door opened, and Abi appeared.

She smiled broadly. "You're here"

"It would appear so" I smiled.

She came out and hugged me.

"I'm so glad you came"

"I'll reserve judgement on that one if you don't mind" I said.

"Of course. You ok?"

"Little nervous"

"You'll be fine. I'll look after you. There's only ten other people here"

"Ten?" That sounded like a lot.

"It's a small flat, could be worse. You look fabulous"

"So do you" She was wearing a knee length black dress with a rose print. And black Converse. Her hair was up in a bun, and her makeup looked lovely.

"I love your shoes" I said.

"Try not to spill your drink on them" she said.

We laughed.

"Come on, let's go up"

She took my hand and lead me up the stairs. The music grew louder as we ascended and entered the living room.

"Everyone, this is Kate"

The people in the room stopped talking and they all directed their gaze upon me. I felt incredibly self-conscious, and squeezed Abi's hand.

"Ok, go back to whatever you were doing" she told them. They all waved and said "Hi", then went back to their conversations.

Thank God.
"Sorry about that, but it had to be done"
"It's ok, I know"
"Let me get that in the fridge" she said, taking the bottle of wine from me. "This looks fancy"
"Oh, it's really not" I lied. It was quite fancy.
"Come on, I'll give you the grand tour"
I smiled, and followed her into the small kitchen.
"The kitchen" she said, gesturing grandly. "Small, but we get by"
She put the wine in the fridge, and took my hand.
We went out into the hallway, and she opened a door
"Bathroom and toilet, just so you know where to go"
She pointed at the other doors. "Mark's room, he's from the north, heart of gold. Niamh's room. Irish girl, accent to die for. And this," she opened a door "Is where the magic happens"
Her room was not at all what I had expected. To be fair, I had no idea what to expect, but this... Wasn't it.
It was spotless. Tidy. Everything in its place.
"Yeah, I know, it's like a show home" she said "Can't help it"
"No, it's wonderful" I smiled "It looks lovely"
The room itself wasn't big, but had enough space for her bed, wardrobe, desk, and an armchair.
It was tastefully decorated, and looked bright and airy.
Not at all what I had expected.
"Your room is lovely" I said.
"Yeah, I know it's not much" she said.
"No, I mean it. It's lovely" I smiled.
"Clean freak isn't to everyone's liking"
"I don't mind" I said.

"How are you feeling?"

"To be honest? A lot better now. I 've been dreading this all day, but it's not actually as bad as I thought it was going to be"

"That's good isn't it?"

"Yes, it is"

She kissed me. "Let's get you a drink"

We went backout to the kitchen and poured two glasses of rosé.

"Right. You ready?"

I nodded.

We went back into the living room, where the people were all moving around rhythmically to a Stereophonics song. The various lamps in the room cast their shadows onto the walls, making it seem alive with dancing shadows.

Abi gripped my hand and took me inside. We stood in the room, and she started moving to the music. I was no stranger to this, so started doing the same. Not like it was dancing, just moving around. It had been a long time since I'd done it in public.

"Hey Abi, who's this?" A guy said, putting his hand on her shoulder. He was flamboyantly dressed, with different coloured nail varnish on each nail. I liked it.

"Mark, this is Kate. I did just introduce her"

"Oh, darling, I've had a few. Forgive me" he said, and kissed my hand. "Pleased to meet you"

"Likewise" I smiled. I was trying to place his accent, but it was heavily disguised in a fabulously gay way.

"The mysterious Kate" he smiled "I've heard about you"

Definitely from the North, but I couldn't quite place it.
"Oh? All good I hope" I said.
"From her? Nothing but the best darling" he said, putting his arm around my shoulder.
"She's quite the catch, you're lucky" he said to Abi.
"Yes, I know" she said, brushing his arm from my shoulder "And she's all mine"
"Spoilsport" he said, feigning upset.
I liked him immediately. He reminded me of Sean.
"Mark here works at the RSC too" Abi explained "See if you can guess where"
He struck a few poses, showing off his outfit.
"Costumes" I chuckled.
"Oh, good guess darling!" he exclaimed.
"You look fabulous" I said "I love your nails"
"Oh these?" he showed his fingers "Expensive, but worth it" he winked.
I laughed nervously.
"You ok?" he asked, looking all concerned.
"I'm a bit anxious around people" I said.
He hugged me "Don't be anxious around me, I love you already. I have a feeling we're going to be great friends"
"I'd like that" I said.
He let me go, and shouted "Hey, time for some decent music"
He walked over to the stereo and flicked through the list on the MP3 player until he'd found what he was looking for. "Aha! Perfect!"
Seconds later, the opening bars to Abba's Dancing Queen blared out of the speakers. The change in music was met with applause in the room.

He immediately went into an obviously well-rehearsed dance routine, and then to my horror, took my hand and pulled me into the middle of the room "Dance with me" he smiled.

"What the hell" I shrugged, and started dancing.

It must be said that I am no dancer, but I moved around to the music just well enough to not make a fool of myself. Abi joined in, and so did everyone else. We were all dancing around, singing along loudly, butchering the classic song. But, nobody cared; they were all lost in the moment. And so was I.

The song was followed by a few more, what you could call gay-disco classics, to which we all danced along. To my utter surprise, I felt completely at ease.

A while, and four glasses of wine later, we were all chatting and having a laugh. I had met everyone in the room, and liked them all. It turned out that Niamh was actually the only straight person in the flat. But, she seemed not to care. "It's a safe environment for a girl on her own" she explained to me. Abi was right; her accent was gorgeous. Words dripped like honey from her Irish tongue. Wow. She wasn't my type though; she had tattoos and a nose stud. I hated tattoos. Sean had tried to get me to have one done, but I had steadfastly refused to foul my body with something I knew I would regret.

Mark was just lovely, and had spent the entire evening looking out for me, making sure I was ok. There was no need, as I was feeling perfectly fine. But, it was really sweet of him.

People started leaving around midnight, which was also my cue to leave; I had work tomorrow.
I booked a taxi on my phone and helped to clear up the living room whilst I waited.
"You did really well" Abi said "I'm proud of you"
"It helped that everyone here is so lovely" I said "Mark is fantastic, he reminds me of Sean"
"Yeah, he's a dream friend" she smiled.
My phone buzzed. "My taxi is here" I said.
It was time to say goodbye. Nerves hit me. What do I do? Kiss her? Just a hug? I wasn't at all sure.
She made up my mind for me, and kissed me. Passionately.
"Wow" I said when she let me go.
"Sorry. Too much?" she asked.
"What? No, it was fantastic"
"Hey, leave some of that for me" Mark said, walking in with some dirty glasses. He put them on the counter and hugged me.
"You are welcome here any time" he said "Don't you dare be a stranger"
"I won't" I said and kissed his cheek.
"Ooh!" he said, fanning his face theatrically with his hands. "She's a hot one"
"Give over you idiot" Abi said, and took my hand. "Come on, I'll see you to your taxi"
"Bye Kate!"
"Bye Mark" I smiled.
We walked down the stairs, and opened the door.
"Just a moment" she said to the driver.
She turned to me, holding my hands "Was it ok?"
"It was great" I smiled "I had such a great time"

"Good" She kissed me again, and lead me to the waiting taxi "I'll see you tomorrow"
"I can't wait" I said.
We waved as the taxi drove away, and then she was out of sight.
I sighed happily. What a fantastic evening.
I had been so worried about it, but it had all turned out rather great. I had made new friends. Me! Making friends!
The driver dropped me off, and I went straight inside, and straight to bed.
Happy.

17. A Perfect Cast of Misfits.

Coffee from Marco's was an absolute Godsend the following morning. I needed caffeine to see me through the morning. I had walked to work in an attempt to wake up a little, but it hadn't really worked. I needed more sleep.
I showed my pass and went up to my office. Silence. Bliss.
The silence didn't last, however, as Jenny appeared after a few minutes.
She was her usual, cheerful self, and we sat for a while, going through the plan for the day. There really wasn't much to do until we got the finalised designs back from the tech guys. In the meantime, I had a team to keep busy.
"Jenny. I'm going to be honest with you. I'm tired. Very tired. My head isn't really in it just yet"
"You want me to keep the team busy?" she asked.
"I guess so, yes"
"No problem, we can go over the structures again to make sure they're right"
"Thanks Jenny"
"No problem" she smiled "You should take the day off, get some sleep"
"No, I can't" I said.
"Why not? We don't have much on until the designs come back. Take a day, chill out"
The idea had merit, I couldn't deny it.
"I'll maybe stick it out till lunch" I smiled.

"Ok, well, if you need anything before then, give me a shout"
"Will do. Thanks Jenny"
She smiled, and left me to the tranquillity of my office. Taking half a day off didn't feel as bad as a fully day. I could last until lunchtime. Couldn't I? Of course. Whilst I had a bit of spare time, I emailed Catherine about Jenny's promotion. I wasn't sure they'd go for it, but what did I have to lose?

I opened up my laptop and started watching *The Winter's Tale*. It was a story of jealousy and infidelity. Or suspicions of infidelity at least. The King, Leontes, exiles his newborn daughter because he thinks she isn't his child. Sad really. But, it all turned out well in the end.

It was, of course, far more complex than that. Deciphering the language Shakespeare used is an art in itself. I had studied it in detail in uni, so was well versed in it. There are, in my opinion, two camps where the language is concerned. The first camp are put off by the language used, as it seems too complicated, or over the top. Too posh. If that's even a thing. They never read Shakespeare because of it. It's too daunting, and trying to understand it? Pah! Nonsense. A small number of these people can be turned by actually going to a theatre and watching a performance. When you see it in person, acted out in front of you, the language combines with the characters and the way they express the verse, the body movements, the inflictions. It's completely different to reading it on a page.

The second camp are snobs. Purists. At the RSC, we sometimes put on productions of Shakespeare that are adaptations, or set in a more modern setting.
These people hate that.
It has to be the way the bard intended! What is this blasphemy? The man would be rolling in his grave! Utter tosh!
Oddly enough, the adaptations and modern interpretations are what brings the first camp closer to Shakespeare. They'll come back to watch more.
And this is exactly what I was using in the curriculum. Bring the kids closer by making it more relatable. They can go on to the classics later, but entice them in by using the modern interpretations.
It had been exactly this that had lured the Chinese in. They could see the potential.
By the time the play had finished, I had made seven pages of notes. Seven! I would compare them to my previous notes some other time, and update the curriculum afterwards.
I checked my phone, no messages. It was, however, just after eleven. I stood and stretched. Ugh, that was enough. Sleep needed. I packed up my stuff and let Jenny know I was leaving.

I bought a bottle of water from the café, and sat out front on the steps. It was a bit overcast today, but it didn't look like it was going to rain at least. There were a lot of people around, and I could see a small queue forming by Shakespeare's statue across the square. His hand was all shiny where people had held it over the years. It was a thing apparently.

A lady was singing away off to my left somewhere, show tunes. Not my favourite, but she had a good voice. Over to the right, the riverboats were packed with people going on their little river cruises.
As with the row boats, the skippers of the river boats had to dodge the plentiful waterfowl on the river. The birds didn't give a damn about the boats, and sometimes refused to get out of the way.
Sadly, the boats wouldn't stop either, and the birds would lose the battle and be pushed aside. It was all very sedate, as the boats chugged along very slowly indeed.
I felt a hand on my shoulder, and jumped a little.
"Sorry darling, didn't mean to startle you"
It was Mark.
"Mark, hey" I said, standing.
"No, let's sit" he said "I do love a bit of people watching"
I sat back down, and he sat next to me. Our legs were touching, but it didn't really bother me.
"How are you princess?" he asked.
"Tired"
"Yeah, me too. I could do with sleeping for a week. But, you know, I'm far too busy being fabulous to sleep"
I giggled "You do it very well"
"Oh, thank you" he said "But I know"
More giggles.
"What are you doing for lunch today?" he asked.
"Lunch? I'm off. I took half a day to chill out"

"Oh, get you!" he said "Sadly, I can't afford to take any more time off. I was just going to head over to the Planetarium café for lunch, if you want to join?"
"Oh, I don't know" I said. "Sit here, or eat fabulous food? Hmmm, tough choice"
He raised his eyebrows "Get you being all funny, girl"
"I'd love to come" I smiled.
"Good" he smiled and took my hand "Come on"
We stood and held hands as we walked the short distance to the café.
The Planetarium was a fashionable Vegan place, totally in with most of the RSC workers. It was *the* place to have lunch.
And, as such, it was rammed when we walked into the small courtyard where it was located. There was a lot of outdoor seating, but it was mostly all taken.
"I have my own table reserved" Mark assured me.
I didn't know if the was joking or not until we walked inside.
"Mark, darling. You're late. I was about to give your table away" A man said from behind the bar.
"Sorry my love" he said walking over. They theatrically kissed cheeks. It was all very flamboyant.
"Lucien, this is Kate, she's Abi's girlfriend"
"Oh, and look at her. Isn't she just lovely" he smiled, taking both my hands. "Very pleased to meet you" he said, kissing my cheek ever so delicately.
"And you" I said.
"Go have a seat, I'll bring you both some water"
We walked out, and sat at the table directly outside the door.
It was set slightly off to the left, against the wall.

Mark picked up the Reserved sign, and placed it off to the side.

"You have a table reserved here every day?" I asked.

"Most days" he smiled "Lucien and I go way back"

"Ex boyfriend?"

"Good God no, I'm far too good for him dear. Just good friends"

I smiled. I liked his company a lot, he was easy to be around, and talked for Britain. Not an ability I was blessed with. Lucien appeared with a carafe of cold water, and set it on the table.

"You having the usual my dear?" he asked Mark.

"Of course darling, its divine"

Lucien smiled at the flattery. "One tries one's best" he said.

"And madame?"

"Ooh, what do you recommend?" I asked.

"Try the Sauerkraut toastie" Mark said, It's delish"

"Sounds good to me" I smiled.

"Coming right up" Lucien said, and disappeared inside.

"How long have you known Abi?" I asked as I poured the water.

"Oh, a few years. She was looking for people to share a flat with, so you know, one thing lead to another, and here we are"

"Going by last night, I take it you all get on very well" I said.

"It's a non-stop party darling" he smiled "There's always people coming and going"

"Sounds like fun" I said "And exhausting"

"Sleep? Ha! You can sleep plenty when you're dead" he said "Live for the moment Kate, life is far too fleeting not to"

I was about to agree with the sentiment, when a thought struck me. I had not been living for the moment. Not for almost three years now. I hadn't been living at all in fact. I'd been surviving, existing. Hiding away from the world had turned me into a recluse. I had forgotten how to be around other human beings, how to act, how to behave. Work was different of course, it was a safe place, and I had no personal connections to anyone there. Well, until now of course.

Now there was Abi, and Mark.

"I'm afraid I've not been doing that" I said quietly.

He took my hand "But you're starting to"

"Yes, I suppose"

"Hey, let me show you something" he said, pulling out his sparkly cased phone. He flicked through until he found what he was looking for.

"Here" he handed me the phone.

It showed a picture of a rather plain looking lad in a hoody and jeans. He looked sad and depressed. His eyes looked hollow, lost.

"This is you?" I asked.

"Eight years ago. My life was a tragic drama, loneliness, isolation, homophobia. My parents were so incredibly angry with me at that time. It was a dark period for me"

"What changed?" I asked, handing back the phone.

"I decided I'd had enough of being sad. I put myself first. I left home and went to Art College in Manchester. I completely changed my appearance, became my true self. I haven't looked back since"
"That sounds very liberating" I said.
"Oh, girl, you have no idea. Being who you were meant to be is such a release. The pressures coming from society to conform can be overwhelming. You just have to have the strength to push them away and be who you want to be"
I took out my phone and showed him a picture of myself in uni.
"Wow, this is you? Look at that fabulous hair! Oh! To die for! And that figure! And that tiny dress!" he fanned his face with his free hand.
"I cut my hair off to spite my mother" I said.
"Why? Look at it"
"I had a friend, he was very much like you. He was called Sean. He sadly died, and my mother was nowhere to be seen. I needed her so badly, but she just didn't have it in her to be a real mother to me. The one thing she was proud of was my hair, so I cut it off"
"Good for you!" he smiled "I bet she hated that"
"Oh, you have no idea. I've kept it short ever since, just to rub it in"
"Wow, you carry a lot of pain" he said.
"Yes, I suppose I do"
"Get us" he said leaning back "Two perfect little misfits"
"I'm growing it back now" I said "It's been long enough"

"You've made up with your mother?"

"Yeah, plus I want to look nice for Abi. And myself"

"Oh, only worry about that last one. Nobody else matters as far as your appearance goes. Abi will love you no matter what"

Love. The word hit me like a brick. He must have noticed, because he quickly added "Love will come with time"

"I know" I said.

"Give it a chance. What have you got to lose?"

"Not much"

"Good. Just let go, and go with the flow"

"I'll give it a try"

18. Circumstances in G Minor.

I said goodbye to Mark after lunch and wandered over the bridge and into the recreation grounds. On impulse, I took a ride on the big wheel. Not something I'd usually consider doing, but I was in a good mood after my time with Mark and had never been on it before.
It was an amazing experience. Not only because of the views it afforded from the top, but also because it stopped at the top for a minute or so. The silence and solitude were just amazing. I was all alone, up here, looking down upon you all. You couldn't hear me if I screamed, and I can't hear the jumbling of voices from below. It was a feeling of complete and utter bliss.
Sadly, it was over all too soon, and I was once more among the masses. I bought an ice cream and sat on the riverside for a while, just watching the world go by.

I was just feeding my last bits of ice cream cone to the swans, when my phone buzzed. I took it out of my pocket and checked; a message from Abi.
Hey, I'm sorry we didn't get together today, I didn't actually make it into work. Not feeling too good. How are you?
I text back: Hey, hope you're feeling better, and it's not too serious. I'm just tired. I took a half day, and ended up having lunch with Mark. He's so lovely.
I was going to press Send, but changed my mind.
I deleted the text and pressed Call instead.

Not something I was known to do. With anyone.
She answered immediately.
"Hey, are you ok? Is something wrong?"
"No, just calling to see how you are. I typed out a text but thought we could talk instead. If you're up to it?"
"Yeah, of course. I'm just feeling a bit icky today, not sure what it is"
"As long as you're ok" I said.
"Yeah, I'm fine. How are you?"
"Tired. I took half a day off, intending to go home and have a nap, but ended up having lunch with Mark"
"Oh, cool. Did he take you to the Planetarium?"
"Yeah, he has like his own table"
"Yeah, Lucien is good to him"
"Oh, he was nice too. And the food was great"
"What did you have?"
"The sauerkraut toastie"
"Yum. Though I couldn't face one right now"
"You poor thing. Are you sure you're alright?"
"I'll be fine, I'll just chill out for the rest of the day, and enjoy the silence of an empty flat. Don't get that opportunity very often"
"Ok, as long as you're sure"
"Yeah, I'm good. Don't worry about me"
"Ok. Well, I'm going to go home and have a long bath. Hopefully see you tomorrow, if not, then soon"
"I'll see how I'm feeling"
"Ok, bye"
"Bye Kate"
I put my phone back in my pocket and walked down the river, towards the weir.
It was less touristy here, and quieter.

Quieter was good, except it brought back the stern words my mother used to drill into me "Never be alone in quiet areas! The world is a dangerous place Kathrina"

I looked around, and decided to turn back. Not that I saw anything untoward, I just... Well, I don't actually know. I just did.

I walked back towards the main road, and onwards to my little castle in the suburbs.

As I turned the corner into my quiet little corner of heaven, I saw it. I couldn't believe it. Surely not. It must be someone else's. But then I saw the number plate. It was definitely theirs. Shit. What were they doing here?

I picked up the pace, and walked up to my house.

They were sat on the grass in the front garden, waiting.

"Ah, there she is!"

"Mum? Dad? What are you doing here?" I asked.

"Oh, nice to see you too Kathrina" my mother said as she got to her feet.

"Hello sweetheart" my dad said, and gave me a big hug. The smell of his aftershave brought back many, many memories of my childhood.

"Hey dad" I said, hugging him back.

"Do I get one of those?" my mother asked, arms outstretched.

"Sure mum" I smiled, and hugged her.

"What are you guys doing here?"

"Well, your father finished in London early, so I thought, what the hell. I want to see my daughter"

"And here we are" dad finished.

"And here you are" I smiled. Inside, I was petrified.

I had no food. What were they going to eat? Do I need to take more time off work? Could I afford to do that? All irrational, of course, but welcome to the anxious brain.

"You ok?" dad asked.

"Yes, of course" I lied "Let's go inside"

"I'll get the bags from the car, you go on in" dad said.

Bags? How long were they planning on staying?

I unlocked the door, and went inside. I picked up the post, and dropped it on the kitchen table. Mum followed me in, and did her best to disguise the fact that she was inspecting my house.

"This is lovely" she smiled.

"It works for me mum" I said, picking up on her sarcasm. She had envisaged her daughter living somewhere far grander than a bungalow in suburban Stratford. And probably already married with kids by now. She had been married at eighteen, and had James a year later. She never tired of reminding me. And telling me that my clock was ticking. Whatever the hell that meant. I was twenty-seven for God's sake, not fifty.

"It's bright and airy" she said "And very clean"

"Yes mum, I know, I'm a clean freak"

"We'll try not to make a mess dear" she assured me.

"It doesn't bother me mum" Which was true. I didn't.

"We thought we'd stay for a few days, if that's ok?"

"Mum, you can stay as long as you like, I don't mind. It's nice to see you"

She went through the cupboards, and then opened the fridge "Well, we'll need to go shopping first I suppose"

"Yes, sorry. If I knew you were coming, I would have got shopping in"
"It's fine dear, we'll drive out to Waitrose and fill your cupboards for you"
I forced a smile "Sounds good, thanks mum"
I didn't shop at Waitrose. In fact, I didn't shop anywhere. I did my shopping online, and had the same order every week.
My mum was a worrier though, and the lack of food in my cupboards had likely shocked her.
"Are you eating ok?" she asked. And…. There it was.
"Yes mum, I eat fine. I'm hardly wasting away"
"Ach" she said dismissively "You take after me thank goodness. You can eat what you want and not put on an ounce"
"Lucky me" I smiled.
"Are you growing your hair?"
"What?"
"Your hair, it's longer than I recall"
"Oh, I don't know. Maybe. We'll see"
"Are you doing it for Abigail?"
"Mother!" I said.
"What's going on?" dad asked, coming in with three bags. Mostly my mother's stuff no doubt.
"Oh nothing" mum smiled. "I was just saying we need to go shopping"
"Oh, of course. I'm sorry Cat, we should have told you we were coming"
"It's fine" I smiled "Shopping sounds fun"
My mother fixed me with a questioning look.
"Ok, not fun maybe"
"We can go on our own?" dad suggested.

"No, it's fine, I'll come. Just let me feed the cat"
"You still have the Tab?" dad asked.
"Yeah, she's around somewhere. Probably asleep"
I sprinkled some food into the cat's bowl, and grabbed my phone.
"Ready"
"Let's go" dad smiled.
I got in the back of dad's midlife crisis mobile, and we set off.
He had always wanted a Porsche, and had insisted it have enough room for all of us, so he had bought a Panamera. I'm not going to lie; it was lush, but not really my style. The car screamed "Hey, you! Look at me!" Not really what I wanted in life.
We drove the short distance to their supermarket of choice, and parked up. Oddly enough, the Porsche didn't stand out here; it fitted in rather perfectly.
I got a trolley, and followed my parents inside. I endured twenty minutes of pure hell, as it was quite busy. Mum insisted on stocking up for me, and by the time we got to the till, the trolley was completely full. There was enough food here to last me six months. I smiled, and thanked her graciously. Even though I didn't really want any of it.
We returned to my little house, and packed away the shopping as best we could. Some of it ended up out in the garage, which was empty save for my bicycle.
I made a pot of tea, and we sat in the lounge.
"Ah, I see you still keep up with your playing" my mum said. My cello was sat in the corner, and had been for a few months now. My cleanfreakness meant it was dust free, giving the impression that it was used.

"Erm, I suppose. I play occasionally" I said.
"Oh Kathrina. Really? You were so good. It seems like a waste to let it go"
My mother had pushed me into playing the cello. I had never wanted to. But, I did eventually grow to love the instrument. However, I rarely played it these days.
My dad gave me a sympathetic smile. He knew the truth.
"So, anyway" he said, changing the subject "How's work?"
"Work is good" I smiled, thankful.
"You got the Chinese to sign on the dotted line" he said proudly.
"Yes, they were most impressed with the curriculum I had presented"
"A great achievement" he said "Well done Cat"
"Thanks dad"
"And how about Abigail?" My mother asked.
"What about her?"
"When do we get to meet her?" she asked impatiently.
"She's not very well at the moment, so I'm not sure"
"Forgive your mother" dad said "She's being rude"
"What? I'm just interested in meeting my daughter's girlfriend"
"Leave it out Hedda" dad said "Give the girl a break"
"Well, I'm just interested" mum maintained.
"I'll see if she's in work tomorrow, maybe we can all have dinner?" I offered. What the hell was I doing?
I had no idea if Abi would even agree to dinner with my parents. Jesus.
I would have to text her and find out.
"Oh, that would be nice, wouldn't it Stephen?"

"Yes, fantastic" dad said. He gave me another apologetic look.

"You have any plans whilst you're here?" I asked, desperate for a change of direction.

"Well, we're at the theatre tonight, but other than that, nothing"

"Oh, you going to see The Constant Wife?" I asked.

"Yes, our friends saw it last week, and it sounded fun" mum said.

"It is" I said "I saw it on opening night; it's very good, you'll enjoy it"

"Are you ok to have dinner alone?" Dad asked, knowing full well that I would be.

"Oh, you're out for dinner?" I asked, pretending to be upset.

"Sorry darling" mum said "We have a table booked in the restaurant before the play"

"Oh, I see. Well, yeah, I'll be fine" I said "Not like there's nothing to eat"

"Still full of wit and sarcasm" My mother said.

"I learned from the best"

"Yes, well I suppose I'd best go and get ready. Can I use the bathroom?"

"Of course mum, help yourself to anything"

She smiled and went off to the spare bedroom to unpack.

"I'm sorry about that my darling" dad said "I'll try to keep her out of your way"

"It's fine dad. Honest. It's nice to see you"

He came over and sat next to me on the sofa.

"How are you?" he asked, putting his arm around me.

"Up and down, the usual"

He kissed my head "I wish I could make it better for you"
"I'll be fine dad. Abi is good for me"
"I'm looking forward to meeting her. Anyone who makes my daughter happy is welcome in my book"
"Thanks dad" What he meant was; *I really don't mind that you're going out with a woman, as long as you're happy.*
"She's really lovely dad" I said.
"Good. It makes me happy to see you finally getting a bit better"
"I think I am. I've made new friends too"
"Excellent, that sounds really positive"
I inwardly cursed myself for sounding like a ten year old, proudly telling her dad she'd made some actual friends. It sounded pathetic. But, that's about where I was at this moment in time.
"Right" he said, standing up "I suppose I'd better go and make sure she's ok"
"Thank you dad"
"For?"
"Everything"
He kissed my head again. "You're my daughter. I'd do anything for you"
He sounded completely sincere. And I knew he was. I didn't really understand the love a parent feels for their child, as I didn't have any. But, I got the idea.

After they'd left to go for dinner, I ran a bath and lay in it for about an hour, trying to de-stress. I was texting Abi throughout, telling her all about the drama.

She was sympathetic, and said she would love to come for dinner if she was feeling better.
I really hoped she would.
My mother would be insufferable else.
I put my phone down and relaxed. I had lit some candles, the cat was curled up on the bathmat, and Chopin's Cello Sonata in G minor was playing away in the background, adding to the feeling of calm.
Everything was as it should be; quiet.

19. Maternal Soliloquies.

I felt too tired to eat after my bath, so I went straight to bed. I had wanted to be in bed before they got back, as I really didn't want to get into a late night conversation about the play. Or worse.
I heard them come in at about half past eleven. It then took me about an hour to get to sleep again. The slightest noise kept waking me.
I woke before the alarm, as usual, and thought for a moment I had dreamed it all. But, I was wrong.
Dad was already up, getting ready to go for a run. Something he'd done three or four times a week for as long as I could remember.
We whispered our good mornings, and he went out.
I went through the rest of my routine, and was ready to walk to work. Today, I wore a nice green dress and sandals.
As much for my own sake, as for my mothers. I didn't want to give her anything to moan about when I got home. Seeing me in a dress would make her happy.
I fed the cat, and quietly left the house. I was free.

I walked straight to Marco's and ordered some scrambled eggs alongside my usual coffee.
"You want food? You sit, I make for you"
"I'm sorry Marco, I don't have time to sit. I'll take it with me if possible"
"Of course signora Kate" he smiled.

I sat in my office and ate the heavenly eggs before going in to see the team. They were all in good spirits, despite the fact that our workload had taken a dip. Jenny was doing a great job at keeping them busy. They had gone over the structures for the different plays, and made a few tweaks. Today they were going to review my notes from *The Winter's Tale* and update them. She would try to have everything ready for review before I went home for the weekend.
Weekend? Shit. It's Friday. That means two days with my parents. Joy. Two days of my mother's criticism.
I thanked Jenny and text Abi to see if she was in work. She was. Yes!
Hey, I'm feeling a lot better thanks, I'm in. We'll see how long it lasts. Let's meet up at lunchtime, I'd like to see you.
She wanted to see me! Wait. Did that mean; I want to speak to you, or just I want to spend time with you? Ugh. Give over already, she just wants to spend time with me. Think positive!
I text back saying I was happy she was better and in work, and would meet her outside. And put a kiss at the end. First time for everything right?

Lunchtime came quickly, and I was almost late.
I'd been watching *A Midsummer Night's Dream*, and was totally engrossed by the naughty Puck weaving his mischievous magic on the unsuspecting Athenian youths.
I slammed my laptop shut, grabbed my bag, and ran downstairs.
Abi was sitting on the steps, waiting.

"Hey, I'm sorry I'm a bit late" I said, all flustered.
She rose to meet me with a hug "I've missed you"
"I've missed you too" I said, holding her tight.
We separated, and held hands as we walked towards the river.
"Feeling ok?" I asked.
"I feel fine, just not hungry" she said.
"I'm glad" I gave her hand a little squeeze.
"How have you been?" she asked.
"Ugh, don't get me started" I said. Not something I thought I'd ever say. Wow.
"That bad eh?"
"My parents are with me all weekend"
"That's great though isn't it?" she smiled. Her beautiful face. Those green eyes. My God she was stunning. All my fears about my mother taking over my life all weekend melted away like snow in the summer sun.
"Yeah, I suppose. It's good to see them. Especially my dad"
"Daddy's girl eh?" she teased.
"I guess so. I've always been closer to him"
"Well, I look forward to meeting them" she smiled.
"You sure? You don't have to you know"
"No, I want to. Just to put your mother's mind at ease if nothing else"
"My mother's mind will never be at ease. You should see the amount of food they bought for me in Waitrose yesterday"
"Waitrose eh? Can't be bad"
"There's too much. Feel free to take whatever you want for the flat after they've gone"
"Ooh, that sounds good"

"I'm happy with what I get for myself, I don't need all that other stuff"
"That's nice of you" she said, and kissed my cheek.
My world lit up instantly.
We found a bench down by the water's edge, and sat.
"I got cannoli from Marco if you're interested" I said, taking them from my bag.
"Tempting" she said.
"It's here if you want it" I said, and took mine from the bag and ate it. Heavenly.
"Not wanting to see Mary today?" she asked.
"I thought we could just sit here. I haven't seen you for so long"
"It's only been two days Kate" she giggled.
"May as well have been two weeks" I said.
"I feel the same" She leaned in and put her head on my shoulder.
"Is your mother really that bad?" she asked.
"Her heart is in the right place, but she's not great at showing emotion or affection. Especially shit at showing affection. She's quite cold sometimes"
"That's unfortunate"
"She is one of six sisters, so I guess attention from nan and grandad was sparse"
"Wow, big family"
"Yeah, it's huge. They're all in Sweden though"
"Thankfully?"
"No, I love my aunties, they're all lovely. I don't know what happened to mum, but she's not like them at all"
"Odd. And she's fine, you know, with us?" She asked.
"Oh God yes, she can't stop telling me how ok they both are with it"

"That's funny. Like she's overcompensating"
"And then some. You'll find out if you come over this evening"
"It will be nice to meet them. And I get to see where you live"
"Number one Waterloo Drive, no secret"
"No, I meant I get to see inside you fool" she said nudging me.
"Ah, yes, of course" I smiled.
She took the cannoli from the bag and devoured it.
"My appetite is returning" she smiled "Must be from being with you"
"I make you hungry?"
She rolled her eyes "That too. I meant you make me better"
"Ah, I see"
We sat for a while, just enjoying each other's company, and then it was sadly time to return to work.
"I'll text you with a time, but I would guess six"
"I look forward to it" she said, and kissed me.
Not just a peck on the cheek, an actual kiss.
She walked away, leaving me standing rooted to the spot. She was all I wanted from life.

I left work at five, after sitting with the team and going through their revisions of my notes. It was all perfect. The walk home was tough; a sense of dread filled me. And it got worse the closer I got to home. This wasn't right. Home was my safe place, not a place to dread.
I was dreading seeing my mother. Her criticisms, comments. She would find something to pick on.
I knew she would.

Dad's midlife crisis mobile was on the drive; they were there. I took a deep breath, opened the front door, and went inside.

"Darling, you're home" mum said, putting her magazine down. She was sitting at the kitchen table with a coffee.
"Yes, I am" I said.
Wait. Something was off here. I smelled something.
"You're cooking?" I asked.
"Yes, I made Sjömansbiff" she smiled "Your favourite"
"With red cabbage?" I asked suspiciously.
"Yes" she smiled "And potato pancakes"
Sjömansbiff is a traditional Swedish sailor's beef stew, and I bloody love it. And red cabbage. And potato pancakes.
What is going on here?
She saw me looking, and rolled her eyes "I just wanted to cook for you, is that so wrong?"
"No, mum, it's quite lovely actually, thank you" I kissed her cheek and sat with her.
"How was work?"
"It was ok, there's not an awful lot to do until they finish the web design proposals next week"
"Oh, I see. Well, I'm sure you're keeping yourself busy"
I knew what she wanted to know; was Abi in today.
I put her out of her misery. "I had lunch with Abi today"
I didn't do lunch, but she didn't need to know that. It would just be something else for her to use against me. Something to analyse.
"A nice red would look nice with your dress" she said.

And so it begins, I thought.
"Red?"
"Nail varnish"
"Oh, I see. I didn't have time to do them last night"
"I could do them for you"
I looked at my nails; they were still painted in the feint pink from the party.
"I was going to wear yellow tomorrow"
"Oh perfect" she said "We'll leave them then"
"What have you been up to today?" I asked, steering attention away from me.
"We went for a nice walk around the town and bought a few things. We had a lovely lunch at the RSC, and then came home"
"You were there? Why didn't you text me? I could have met you"
"With Abigail?" she asked.
"Yes, she was back in work today. We spent our lunch break on a bench by the river"
"How lovely" she said. "Does that mean she'll be joining us for dinner? I made enough"
"Of course you did" I smiled "I'll text her"
"Oh you kids and your texts. Whatever happened to telephone calls?"
My turn to roll my eyes. I picked up my phone and text Abi: Dinner is on. Six ok for you?
She text back immediately: *Look forward to it!*
Oh, little do you know!
"She'll be here at six" I said.
Mum clapped her hands together in excitement.
"Fabulous. I'll go get ready"
Get ready? For what?

I decided not to ask, and just let her get on with whatever she had planned. It was better that way.
Dad came in from his run, all hot and out of breath.
"Hello angel" he smiled. He held out his arms to hug me, all sweaty and horrible.
"Ugh! Have a shower first" I chuckled.
I loved my dad. He always knew exactly what to say and do to make me happy. My parental rock.
"I assume your mother is getting ready? Does that mean Abi is joining us?"
"Yes, she is" I smiled.
"It'll be nice to meet her" he said "I'll try to control your mother, but I can't promise anything"
"I know, it's fine. What is she getting ready for?" I asked.
"She's dressing for dinner" he explained.
"Shit"
"Yep. Shit. I have to wear trousers and a shirt"
"Oh God. I'd better go get ready myself then. I was just going to wear shorts and a tee"
"Same here. But, you know your mother. She wants to impress"
"I'd better warn Abi"
"Yes, that would be a good idea"
He went off to shower, and I text Abi in a mild state of panic. It was just before five already. Would she have time to dress for dinner?
I text her: Hey, just found out mum is dressing for dinner. Just to pre-warn you. I'm wearing a dress.
I was going to dress nicely anyway to meet your parents, so no drama.
I was just going to wear shorts and a tee.

That would be nice, but we should try keep your mother happy.
Thank you. I should probably warn you that my mum has a tendency to speak her mind.
No prob, see you soon. X.
Relieved, I rushed to the bedroom to get myself ready. I was relieved that Abi was already dressing up, not about my mother speaking her mind. I hoped she'd reign it in a bit and not upset Abi.
Stress!

Oh God. No.
I came out of my room, and found my mother in the kitchen. She looked stunning.
Her white blonde hair was done in a halo braid, like a crown around her head. Her makeup was immaculate, and she wore a black cocktail dress with heeled shoes.
I, on the other hand, was wearing a lime green, knee length wrap dress with white flowers on it. And, of course my short hair, minimal makeup, and sandals.
I looked perfectly plain in comparison.
"Can I help, mother?" I asked.
She looked up, and I could see the disappointment in her eyes. It wasn't the clothing. It was my hair. It had been her pride and joy, and I had hurt her deeply when I had it cut off.
"I know" I said "I'm growing it back, don't worry"
She forced a smile and asked me to set the table.
Dad joined me wearing his trademark chinos and white shirt.
"Don't worry about her" he said "She'll get over it"
"I wanted to hurt her. That's why I did it" I said.

"You have no idea Cat. You're her only daughter, and she was so proud of you"
"Was?"
"Poor choice of words. She still is. You know what I meant"
"I'm sorry I didn't live up to her image of the perfect daughter"
"Have you maybe tried telling her that?"
"No"
"Give it a try. Not now though, leave it till tomorrow"
"Ok"
"I got wine. Thought you'd need it" he smiled.
"How many bottles?" I joked.

Six o'clock was fast approaching, and my nerves steadily increased accordingly.
I decided at the last moment to take one of my pills to try keep myself in check.
"You're still on the Propranolol?" Mum asked.
"Yes mum"
"Does it still work for you?"
"I don't take it all the time, only when I need it"
"And tonight is one of those occasions?"
"Yes mum. I'm nervous"
"I'm sure she's just lovely" she offered.
"No, I'm nervous about you"
"Me?"
"I just want this to go well mum, please don't comment negatively on her appearance or anything"
"I had no intentions of doing so" she said defensively.
"I'm just nervous. Let's have a good evening?"
"Ok, well, I'm sure it'll be fine" she smiled.

I shook my head and went out into the front garden to get some air.

I sat on the bench by the front door, with the cat rubbing against my legs.

"Oh Tabs, I hope this goes ok" I said.

As I did so, a taxi pulled up.

Abi was here!

I jumped up and walked out to meet her.

She got out of the taxi and gave me a smile "Hi"

"Hi"

She looked stunning. If I thought my mother looked good, this was next level. A mixture of relief and joy filled my heart.

"You look fantastic" I said.

Her long brown hair was done up in a bun, and she wore a lovely midnight blue dress and flat, black shoes.

I resisted the urge to kiss her as I didn't want to mess up her perfect makeup.

"Come on in" I smiled.

I nervously took her hand and lead her inside. My parents were standing by the kitchen table, like royalty.

Here goes nothing.

"Mum, dad, this is Abigail" I said.

My dad was obviously the consummate gentleman and nice person. "Very pleased to meet you Abigail" he said, smiling.

"And you Mr Harrington"

"Please, call me Steve" he said, smiling "Mr Harrington makes me sound old"

Good for you dad, I thought.

Mum, was still sizing her up as he did so.

I couldn't tell what she was thinking. I only hoped it was positive.

"Nice to meet you" Mum said. Then, much to my surprise, added "You're even more beautiful than Kathrina makes you out to be"

"Oh, thank you Mrs Harrington" she said, blushing.

"Likewise, call me Hedda" she smiled.

Abi nodded, and handed me a bottle of rosé.

"Thanks" I smiled "I'll put it in the fridge"

"I'll do that" dad said "Why don't you show Abigail around"

I looked at Abi. A tour? I live in a bungalow?

"Sure" I took her hand "Come"

Mum and dad went to the kitchen, leaving the two of us alone.

I walked her out into the back garden.

"You ok?" I asked.

"I'm fine" she smiled "They're lovely"

"Hmmm. My mother is up to something, I can feel it"

"You worry too much. Nice garden"

"Low maintenance" I smiled.

"It's perfectly lovely"

My garden was not huge, but not tiny either. I had no grass to cut, as most of it was paved. There were some lavender plants in full bloom, and a few others whose names I don't know. I had two sitting areas; one in the sun and one in the shade. A small water feature added to the sense of tranquillity.

"Come, I'll show you around inside"

Inside, I showed her the lounge, the spare room, bathroom, my office, the kitchen/utility room, dining room, and finally, my bedroom.

"And this is where the magic happens" I smiled as we went in.
"Ah, good one" she said. It's very nice Kate, very clean"
"Yeah, I know, it's like a show home I can't help it"
Again, the exact words she had used in her flat.
"You're funny. I see we have something else in common then"
"Fastidious cleaning?" I joked.
We both laughed, and sat on the bed.
"Nice mattress" she said.
"Oh, erm, thanks. Hybrid I guess"
"It's comfy" she smiled. "There's lots of space here, looks deceptive from the outside"
"Because it's a bungalow? I think the dormer rooms and rear extension help" I took her hand "Thanks for coming"
"It was never in doubt. And, don't worry about your mum, I can look after myself"
"I know, she just makes me nervous"
"It'll be fine. Let's get a glass of wine"
We returned to the kitchen, where mum was busy putting the final touches to the feast she had created.
"Hope you're hungry" she smiled.
"Very much so, it smells lovely" Abi said.
"Traditional Swedish recipes" mum said proudly.
"I look forward to trying them" Abi smiled.
"Good. Why don't you girls go and sit. We'll serve dinner"
"I'll get the wine" I said.
I took a bottle of red and a rosé, and headed back into the dining room.

We sat at the table, and I poured wine for all of us. Red for the parents, and rosé for us girls.

"Here's hoping it goes ok" I said, raising my glass.

"It'll be fine. Cheers"

"Cheers"

Mum and dad joined us and served up dinner.

My goodness, it was delicious. I hadn't eaten this well for a long time.

"This is delicious Mrs Harrington" Abi said.

"Thank you" mum smiled "That's very kind of you to say"

"She's right mum. It's lovely"

"Well, you could have it more often if you ever came to visit"

And so it began. Mum speaking her mind. Joy of precious flippin' joys.

Dad caught my eye and shook his head slightly; don't bite.

"Well, it's nice regardless" I said.

"So, Abigail. Kathrina tells me you work in production?"

"Yes, that's right" Abi said "I'm busy with our winter season production at the moment"

"Ah, how nice" mum smiled "And you work as a production assistant?"

"I started as a production assistant, now I'm one of the Production Supervisors"

"That sounds exciting" mum said.

"It very much is" Abi continued "I supervise the various artistic directors for *The Winter's Tale*"

"Must be fascinating" dad said, trying to be more positive than mum.

"Oh it is" Abi smiled "It's quite the job to get everything organised and constructed. Some of the set designs can be very technical"

"I bet" dad smiled. "We went to see *The Constant Wife* last night, it was fantastic wasn't it Hedda?"

"Oh yes, it was wonderful" mum said "So funny"

"My friend Mark did the costumes for that one" Abi said "What did you think?"

"The girls outfits were just perfect" mum said "I loved them"

"Oh, that's good, I'll pass that on. He'll be delighted to hear it" Abi said.

"Do you live in the area?" mum asked. Another loaded question, to find out how well off Abi was no doubt.

"Yes, I live in town. I share a flat with Mark and an Irish girl, Niamh, who does makeup at the RSC"

"Sounds great" dad said "Plenty of parties eh"

"Yes" Abi smiled "There are plenty of good times"

"Not too good I hope?" Mum cut in.

"We're all responsible adults Mrs Harrington. We work hard and play respectfully"

"Ha! I like that" dad said "Play respectfully"

"Yes quite" mum said sour faced. "Are you from the area originally?" Was the next question. Have to find out what the socio-economic background is...

"No, I'm from Salisbury originally"

"And you came here to work at the RSC?"

"Dream job. I mean, who wouldn't?"

Mum looked at me and said "Yes, who wouldn't"

She had seriously wanted me to go to Oxford and become a Professor there. But, I had disappointed her yet again by moving here.

"And how long have you liked girls exactly?" mum asked.

"Mum!" I shouted.

Dad almost spat out his wine "Hedda!"

Abi giggled "It's ok, honestly. It's actually a good question. To which I can only answer that I don't know. I mean, how long have you been into women Mr Harrington?" she said, turning to dad.

"Me? Oh, well, let's see. Erm, I don't know. Probably from around age eleven or twelve I suppose? There was this girl in year six, Colleen Grimshaw…"

"Yes, that's quite enough of that thank you Stephen" mum cut in.

"To answer your question, Mrs Harrington, I had my first… experience aged sixteen"

"Experience?" mum asked, looking shocked.

"I kissed a girl" she explained.

"Oh, well, we've all done that dear" she said, smiling.

"Mother!" I exclaimed, shocked. Dad just stared at her in amazement.

"What? We've all been young Kathrina" she winked.

My mother. Prim and proper Hedda Harrington, kissed a girl? This was turning out to be quite the evening. Dad looked at her, and I could see the gratitude and admiration in his eyes. She had turned the evening around, and he was proud of her.

He took her hand and squeezed it gently.

"That's good to know dear" he said, smiling.

"Well, what can I say, year ten girls team hockey trip to Malmö"

"Mother!" I said out of pure amazement. "Too much detail"

"What? Ingrid was such a devastatingly good looking girl. How could I resist?"
"Oh my God, mother" I gasped.
"Look, what I'm trying to say is I'm fine with it" mum explained.
"In a roundabout way" dad added.
"You can say that again" I said "Jesus"
"Are you planning on staying the night?" she asked Abi as she topped up her wine.
"Oh God" I said, hiding my head in shame.
Dad just laughed and shook his head.
"Erm, well I haven't brought anything, so wasn't planning on it" Abi said, a bit flustered.
"Anyone for dessert?" mum asked, grinning broadly.
"You made desert?" I asked, amazed.
"Just Semlor, nothing special"
"Semlor?" Abi asked.
"Rolls, filled with almond paste and fresh cream" dad explained.
"And a bowl of warm milk to dip them in" I added.
"Sounds intriguing" Abi said "Can I help with anything?"
"Oh, good idea" Mum said "You come with me, we'll prepare it together"
"Oh, erm…" I said, trying to stop this disaster from happening.
"Ach, relax Kathrina. You catch up with your father for a moment"
The two of them went off to the kitchen, leaving dad and I at the table.
"This isn't good" I said.
"She'll be fine Cat. She likes her"

"She does?"

"When is the last time your mother let *anyone* help her in the kitchen?"

He was right. The kitchen was mum's territory, and she never let anyone help her. This was interesting. And a very good sign indeed. Even I hadn't been allowed to help my mum. Well, I did when I was small, but not since.

"She sure is full of interesting revelations this evening isn't she?" I chuckled.

"Yes, who'd have thought it eh?"

"Quite. She's the last woman on earth I would have suspected to have kissed another girl"

"Me too, believe me"

"Maybe we should limit her wine intake from here on in" I said.

"Ach, leave her. I haven't seen her this relaxed in ages. It's good for her to unwind occasionally"

"Just so you know, Abi isn't staying over. That was never the plan"

"Cat, your house, your rules. Do whatever you please"

"Thanks, but it wasn't even mentioned ok?"

"Sure" he smiled.

"Right, make room" mum said, returning with a large plate full of delicious looking buns, dusted in icing sugar.

Abi had a large bowl of warm milk for us all to dip our rolls into.

It was both messy, and delicious.

Later, we had done the dishes, and were sitting in the lounge, chatting about James and his new girlfriend.

Shit. I hadn't mentioned to mum about Christmas.

"Oh, erm I forgot to tell you mum, we're going over to see James for Christmas this year"

I winced as I finished, anticipating a barrage of emotionally laden abuse. But, to my surprise, none came.

"Oh, yes, your dad mentioned. We're going skiing with Jurgen and Annie"

My auntie Ana was my mother's dearest sister. They got on very well indeed. As did dad and Jurgen… they were just happy to have each other as drinking partners.

"Ah, that sounds perfect" I said "Christmas in the snow"

"Yes, I'm rather looking forward to it actually" mum said "We haven't really had a Christmas free ever"

"I'm sure you'll have the best fun" I said.

Abi had remained silent during this discussion, as she knew it could have been a touchy subject. But, true to form, mum dragged her into it anyway.

"How do your parents feel about your going Abigail?"

"Oh, I have no idea. I'm not close to my parents"

"What? Whyever not?"

I was as shocked by this as my mum. We had spoken about her parents, but she hadn't told me they weren't talking.

"Oh, you know. They were disappointed they wouldn't get grandkids. Add to that the embarrassment I caused them"

"Oh, what nonsense!" mum exclaimed "That's what turkey basters are for"

"Mother!" I shouted.

"I'm joking" she smiled. "But, it's an option"
"I'm sure it's moved on a bit more since our day dear" dad said.
"Yuck, I'd hope so" I said.
"Anyway, it's a real shame Abigail. I can't imagine ever not talking to my lovely Kathrina"
"Lovely?" I said, surprised.
"Yes. Lovely" she smiled.
"I'm ok with it now" Abi said "I wasn't for the longest time. I hated them for disowning me. But, now, I just feel sorry for them"
"Good for you" mum said. "If you ever need someone to talk to, give me a call"
"Professionally or emotionally?" I mocked.
"Oh Kathrina, really. I'm just trying to be nice"
"It's very kind of you Mrs Harrington" Abi said "I appreciate it"
"And I think on that note, that it's time for us to go to bed" dad said.
"But it's still early Stephen" mum protested.
"Let's leave the girls in peace for a while shall we?"
"Oh, very well" she conceded, and got up.
She held out her arms "Goodnight darling" she said.
I hugged her. "Goodnight mum, and thanks for a wonderful, if eventful, evening"
"My pleasure" she smiled.
"Goodnight Abigail, nice to have finally met you"
"And you Mrs Harrington"
"Night Cat, night Abi"
"Night dad"
"Goodnight Mr Harrington. Sorry, Steve"
He smiled, and dragged mother off to the bedroom.

"Wow" I said, as we fell down onto the sofa.
"Wow indeed" Abi said "Your mum is quite a character"
"That's putting it mildly. Though, she does like you"
"You think so?"
"I know so"
"Well, that's good isn't it?"
"Yeah, it is. Very good"
"Just to put your mind at ease, I hadn't even contemplated staying over" she said.
"I know, it's fine. Just my mother stirring the pot"
"I'll order a taxi" she picked up her phone and did as such. I almost stopped her, but saw sense in the end. It would be the alcohol asking her to stay, not me.
Her taxi came five minutes later, and I walked her out.
"Thanks for coming" I said, holding her hands.
"I'm glad I did, it was great" she said.
My inhibitions compromised, I leaned in and kissed her. A lingering kiss.
She didn't resist, instead just went along with it. It was nice. Warm, and loving.
Reluctantly, I let her go, and she disappeared into the waiting cab.
I sighed, and went back inside to tidy up before going to bed.
What an evening. My mother! Jesus. I still couldn't believe it. But, she had really made an effort tonight, and I loved her for it.
She liked Abigail.
That made me happy. Stupidly happy.

20. Metamorphosis in Pink.

Oh my God. My head. I need water. Asap. I crawled out of bed, slowly, painfully.
Mum and dad were sitting at the kitchen table, cheerfully chatting away.
"Jesus, how do you do that?" I asked, shielding my eyes from the sunlight filtering in through the window.
"A pint of water before bed, remember?" dad said.
It had been something he had drilled into me in my teenage years. Hydrate before going to bed.
"Yeah, I may have forgotten"
"Just you for breakfast?" mum asked.
I rolled my painful eyes "Yes"
"Shame. Such a nice girl"
"Too early mum" I said, holding up a hand to stop he. I left them laughing, and disappeared off to have a lukewarm shower to try wake myself up.

I felt better after, and decided to dress up nicely to try and at least look nice outwardly today. I had bought a nice faded pink floral dress. It would do nicely.
"Oh my, look at you" mum said as I reappeared.
"Just a dress mum"
"Pink. Oh! My girl is back"
"I never went away" I said, popping two paracetamol.
"You know what I meant" she said "Anyway, fancy going out for breakfast?"
"Not really, I'm still pretty full from last night"
"Yes, me too" dad complained.

"Oh, ok, maybe just a coffee then? And maybe a Danish? You know somewhere nice?"
"I know the perfect place" I smiled.

"Oh mama mia!" Marco shouted as I walked in "La bella signora Kate, and on a Sabato!"
"Morning Marco" I smiled.
"You are looking delicate. Party last night?"
"Just dinner" I said. "Hey, these are my parents"
"Caspita! This bella signora is your mama? No! She is too young"
"You're a real smoothie Marco" I chuckled.
He theatrically kissed mum's hand, who was in complete awe.
"And this is papa" he said, hugging dad. Dad was a bit taken aback, but went along with it.
"You want breakfast? Cappuccino?"
"Mum likes Danish" I suggested.
"Ah, signora, you come with me, I show you"
He took mum's hand and lead her over to the pastries.
"Quite the character" dad said, as we sat at a table.
"He's lovely dad" I said "Completely harmless"
Mum returned with a large almond croissant, and a smile to match.
"He's a proper charmer" she said.
"He's lovely isn't he?" I smiled.
"Here we go" Marco said, coming over with a tray.
"Three finest cappuccino"
"Thank you Marco" I said.
"Where is signora Abigail?" he asked.
"In bed if she had any sense" I said "We had a late night"

"Oh, I see" he winked.
"Marco!" I said "I'm not that kind of girl"
"Sure" he smiled. "You have a good day, I gotta go to wholesalers"
"You too, thank you Marco" I kissed his cheek.
"Oh! Mama mia!"
After breakfast, mum and dad went off to walk around the town, leaving me free to do whatever I wanted with my day. I sat by the river and text Abi.
Hey, you up?
Hey, yeah, I'm just on my way to Marco's for a coffee. You free?
Wow! We've literally just left there.
We?
Mum and dad. They've gone off for a walk, so I'm at a loose end…
Not for long. Where are you?
By the Hamlet statue.
I'll be there in ten. X.

I sat in the sun and sipped my coffee. It was starting to get busy, and I soon found myself surrounded by tourists. Fortunately, Abi came to my rescue.
"My hero" I said, rushing over to her.
"My, my, don't you look nice" she said, admiringly.
"Well, you know, one likes to make an effort"
"Puts me to shame"
"You look lovely" I assured her.
She was wearing grey leggings and a long green tee, with yellow trainers. Lovely.
"What do you want to do?" she asked.
"How about the butterfly house?"

She laughed "You know what, I've never been"
"Well, first time for everything" I smiled "Come on"
We held hands as we fought our way through the crowds on the bridge, and I paid for us to get in.
"My treat" I smiled.
We went inside, and were instantly hit by a wall of heat and humidity.
"Oh wow" Abi said.
"Yeah, it's a bit hot, forgot to mention"
Despite the heat, it was pretty busy inside, adding to the discomfort. We walked around for about half an hour, spotting as many butterflies as we could. There were some huge blue ones which glided around the place without fear.
"Look at that one!" Abi said, pointing to a beautiful bright green one, floating towards us. It came to rest on my dress, drawn by the colour.
"Oh my" I said as it crawled around on my bosom.
"I'll get rid of that for you if you like" Abi joked.
"Sure" I said, slowly turning to face her.
She held out her hand, enticing the beautiful creature from its false landing place.
"Come on you, those are mine" she said as the confused butterfly crawled onto her hand. She gently lifted her arm and let it fly off to find real flowers.
"Yours?" I asked.
"Well, you know" she shrugged.
"Ooh look" I said, spotting a birthing rack behind her.
"Are those cocoons?" she asked.
"They tend to call them chrysalis, not cocoons" I said.
"Oh, ok, forgive me" she chuckled.

"Fascinating isn't it? Caterpillar goes in, and a beautiful butterfly emerges"
"A wonderful transformation" she said "Like you, my beautiful pink butterfly"
"Oh, give over!" I said, laughing. "Come on, let's go get some fresh air. The hot air is obviously getting to you"
We went outside where it was blissfully cool. Well, cooler than in there anyway.

21. THE ANGEL OF FONDNESS.

I took Abi for lunch at the Planetarium, where we discussed our plans for Christmas.
We'd be going for a week, which was enough to be honest. I'd like to spend more time with James, but at the same time, didn't want to overstay my welcome. It was nonsense of course, James wouldn't mind if we stayed for a month. It was just me. I didn't like putting people out. Plus, he was in a new relationship, so I didn't want to inject any potential strain there either.
"What goes on behind the mask?" Abi asked.
"Pardon?"
"Just wondering, you've been sat there thinking for a while. Just wondering what goes on"
I explained my logic regarding us staying at James's house.
"It's all superfluous" she said "We only get a week off anyway"
She was right. Curse my mind!
"To save your worries, try using me as a sounding board"
"I'd be on the phone to you all the time" I said "You wouldn't want that"
"Kate. We're supposed to be in a relationship. Of sorts. We're supposed to be there for each other"
"A relationship *of sorts*?" I didn't like the sound of that, it sounded far too casual for my liking.
"You know what I mean, taking it slow, all that. Not that we're *not* in a relationship"

"I see. That's fine then"
"You're still worried" she said.
"Yes"
"If nothing else, by spending time with you, I'm getting a far better insight into how your mind works" She smiled.
I could feel tears welling up in my eyes. Damn my mind!
"Hey, no need to get upset over it" she said, placing her hand over mine.
"I can't help how my mind is" I said, close to tears.
"You don't have to worry about that around me. Just talk to me. I'm here to try help"
"I feel like a child" I said "In desperate need of help all the time"
"You're no child" she said "You're a beautiful woman"
"I don't feel like a woman"
"I can change that" she winked.
"Are you very experienced?" I asked, my logical brain kicking in.
"What? Well, no, maybe not. I mean, I've had a girlfriend before, but that was a long time ago"
"And you had sex?"
"I like to call it making love. Sex sounds so seedy and clinical. But, yes, we did. A couple of times"
"What's it like?"
"Have you never had sex before?" she asked, frowning slightly.
I could feel the blood rushing to my face. Nobody had ever asked me that.
"Erm, no. I haven't"
"Not even with a bloke?"

I pulled a face that said it all.

"Yeah, I feel the same" she said.

"No I feel even more like a child"

"I'm only marginally more experienced than you, so it's not that bad" she smiled. "Besides, I like the idea"

"Of me being a virgin?"

"Ugh, such an ugly name for it. Of you being inexperienced"

"Are you sure? It doesn't put you off?"

"Why would it put me off?" she asked. "Ah, no, wait. It's your mind telling you you're not good enough, isn't it? I thought we had this conversation?"

"We did"

"Look Kate, like I said, if anything you're too good for me, not the other way around"

"I know" I said.

"You know? What? You know you're too good for me? You cheeky sod!"

We laughed, and finished our lunch. We decided to take a walk along the river, up to the church.

This was both a novelty and a scary experience at the same time. I had never spent a day with someone else before. Well, not like this anyway. I was used to being on my own. What would we do for the rest of the day? Were we going to spend all day together?

"What's on your mind?" she asked as we walked.

"I was just thinking about us spending the day together. Are we going to spend the whole day together? What will we do? I've never done this before"

"You've never spent a day with anyone?"

"Not with someone I'm..." I said, but stopped short of actually saying the words aloud.

"I'm...?" she asked.

We sat down on the grass opposite the Dirty Duck. "Listen. Before I say it, understand that I struggle to know what it means. It's not something I've experienced before"

"You know, you could have saved yourself by just saying someone I'm fond of, like we agreed on"

"Shit"

"Look Kate. You may not know what it is in your mind, but your heart does. You don't have to say it, not just yet. It's a bit too soon. We need to get to know each other better, and we do that by spending time together"

"I'm very fond of you" I smiled.

"And I of you" she said, and kissed me.

"Thanks for saving me" I said.

"We're here to save each other"

"My Chanel angel" I smiled.

"Only because you bought it for me"

"It suits you"

"Oh, I know" she chuckled. "What do you feel like doing?"

"Other than..."

"Yes, other than that" she smiled.

"I don't know. What do you usually do?" I asked.

"Oh, you know, the usual. Gym, shopping, cleaning, laundry"

"Sounds similar to my day, I would maybe go for a run, no gym for me"

"Run? As in jogging?"

"Yes"

"Around here?"

"Sometimes, mostly on the other side of the river"

"Can I join sometime? I'd like to give it a go"

"Sure, you have shoes?"

"Running shoes? No, gym shoes"

"What size are you?"

"Five and a half"

I smiled "I'm a six. You can use a pair of mine if you just want to try it"

"Won't they be too big?"

"Nope, you'll be fine"

My phone buzzed.

"My parents. Do you want to go out for dinner tonight?"

"Where?"

"Dunno. Probably somewhere nice though. You'd be doing me a favour, and they'll be paying…"

"I'm in" she smiled.

"Great, thank you"

I text mum back saying we'd love to. I had no idea where we'd be going, but I knew it would be expensive.

"Will we have time to go for a run before dinner?" she asked.

"Oh, yeah. We won't be eating till about seven"

"I guess I'll need to dress up?"

"Yeah. Definitely. We can pick up your stuff and you can get ready at mine if you like?"

"Good idea"

We walked over to her flat, and she packed a bag.

The place was deserted and quiet. Is she here alone every weekend? I thought. That's not good.

"Everyone out?" I asked.

"Yeah, Niamh goes to her sister's in Gloucester every weekend, and Mark has gone to some concert or other in Bristol"

"Nice and quiet?"

"Yeah, doesn't happen often" she smiled.

22. Above us, the Stars.

We walked to my house after collecting her stuff, and got ready to go for a run. It was then that she's discovered she'd forgotten her workout gear.
"What do you wear?" she asked.
I opened a drawer and threw some running shorts on the bed.
"These usually"
She held up the lycra shorts "These? Bit revealing aren't they?"
I blushed.
"I'm joking" she smiled. "And on top?"
"Just an old tee"
"You have a spare sports bra?"
"Erm, yeah, sure" I did, but her bust was larger than mine. Do I mention it or just give it to her?
I pulled one out of the drawer and handed it to her.
"Might be a bit small, cup size I mean"
"I'm sure I'll manage just this once" she said, smiling.
"Ok, well, I'll leave you to get changed" I said, and went out to the kitchen to get a bottle of water.
I didn't have to leave her to get dressed in private of course, I could easily have stayed. But, I would have felt uncomfortable doing so. Don't get me wrong, I'd been in girls changing rooms at school and stuff. However, this is different: I fancy her.

After fetching the water, I went to the bathroom and changed. I checked in the mirror, and she was right; the shorts were very revealing. But, I had researched; this is what normal women wore to run in.

I felt self-conscious now. Thankfully, my tee was long enough and mostly covered my backside.

Abi was in the kitchen waiting when I emerged from the bathroom.

"Bit tight, but not too uncomfortable" she said, referring to the sports bra.

"It looks fine" I said. "Give me a twirl"

She did so.

"Ah, yeah, you're right. The shorts are a little revealing"

"Oh, really?" she said, turning around. "Hmmm, a little maybe"

Tease.

"Right, shall we stretch?" I said, trying not to blush.

"This just gets worse" she giggled.

We managed to stretch without further innuendos, and went out to start our run.

"Right, we'll head down to the park, go around for a bit, then head back. All flat, it'll be fine"

"Ok coach" she smiled "Lead the way"

I prepped my watch, and started the run.

We ran down the main road, and on towards the river. The park was pretty busy with tourists and families enjoying the sun. You could easily spot the people who were walking home from work, as they stood out in their work clothes, looking all hot and bothered.

"You ok?" I asked as we were about half way around the route I'd imagined.

"Yeah, not bad"

Her work in the gym meant that she had a good level of fitness, and was less tired than she would have been otherwise.

"You think you can manage five k? We've just done three"

"Yep, I'll be fine"

We trotted on, reaching the 5k mark before leaving the park. That meant we had the walk home to cool down a bit.

"That's a good time, considering you don't run" I said, showing her my watch.

"I'll take your word for it. What's your normal time?"

"Just under a minute faster, not much" I said.

"Glad not to have held you back then" she smiled.

"You don't hold me back" I said "Quite the opposite"

"Water?"

"Oh yes, please, I'm sweating like mad"

I handed her the bottle, and she drank half of it down in one go.

"Ah, better" she smiled, handing the bottle back to me.

"Thanks for taking me out, I enjoyed that"

"My pleasure"

Mum and dad were home when we got back, and were sitting out in the back garden.

I sat with them whilst Abi went for a shower.

"You're not joining her?" mum asked.

I gave her a look.

"Just asking" she said.

"No, I'm not. Where are we going for dinner?"

"Oh, nowhere crazy, just Loxley's" dad said.

That was a relief. Loxley's was expensive, but not super expensive and formal. Good. Probably dad's choice.
"Oh, that's good, I like it there"
I could clearly see from the look on mum's face that she had wanted to go somewhere a bit more upmarket. Good for dad, he had probably put his foot down.
"Are you sure it's ok for Abi to come?" I asked.
"Of course, why wouldn't it be?" mum asked.
"No reason, just asking"
"Hadn't you better go have a shower?" mum said, pulling a face.
"I'll go see if she's done" I smiled, and walked to the bathroom. The door was open, meaning she had indeed finished. Grateful, I got in and had a nice cold-ish shower, then washed my hair.
I wrapped in a towel, and went to my bedroom.
Abi was sat on the bed doing her makeup. In her underwear.
"Oh, I didn't realise you weren't finished" I said apologetically.
"I'm sure you've seen a girl in underwear before" she said.
"Of course, but not one I fancied" I smiled.
"Oh is that so" she said, turning to me.
"Yes"
"Lucky me" she winked, and returned to her makeup.
"Don't mind me, get yourself ready"
"Oh, of course" I said. I wasn't at all comfortable. But, I just did it anyway. I managed to stay hidden behind the wardrobe door whist I dried off.
Abi was by that time fully dressed and ready to go.

She turned and asked if she should go sit with my parents. I blushed hard, as I was stood in my underwear.

"Oh, erm, yeah, if you want"

"You're funny" she winked "I'll leave you to it"

She looked me up and down, then smiled and left. I felt exposed.

I was pretty sure that I shouldn't feel that way, but I did anyway. What did that mean? Surely I wasn't supposed to feel uncomfortable around Abi, regardless of my level of decency.

Was this how normal women felt?

Probably not. They probably wouldn't care. But me? Ugh. And now this meal? I hoped mum behaved herself tonight. She seemed to like Abi, and I really hoped I wasn't wrong.

I did my makeup and put on my blue dress.

Time to face the music. Whatever that meant.

"Ah, there you are" mum said, "We need to leave darling or we'll be late"

"Just put these in the wash" I said "Two minutes"

"But the taxi..." she said, then sighed.

I put the running clothes in the machine, and started it up.

"Ok, ready" I smiled.

Mum looked at her watch impatiently. In her opinion, one should always be at least ten minutes early for any appointment. I obviously did not live by such rules.

The taxi dropped us at the restaurant at two minutes to seven. Perfect in my book.

Mum huffed and puffed like a hard done by teenager as we went inside.

We were met by a young lady who took us to our table.

Dad ordered wine; red and rosé, and we perused the menu whilst the waitress got our wine.

"What do I have" Abi whispered.

"Starter, main, and desert. Desert is optional" I said quietly. "And don't worry about the price"

Under the table, our legs touched. I felt instantly at ease.

The waitress returned and offered the wine. Dad tasted the red, and nodded his approval. I tasted the rosé and did likewise.

Rather unfairly, mum suggested Abi order first as she was our guest.

Fortunately, she didn't disappoint.

"Oh thank you Mrs Harrington. I'll have the seared scallops to start and the fillet steak, medium with broccoli and harissa"

"Nice choice" dad smiled "I'll have the same. I love scallops"

I ordered the feta and pistachio feta spring rolls to start and the seabass for my main. Mum also chose the scallops, and had the rib eye, medium for her main.

"Well, that all sounds rather lovely" mum said, and raised her glass "A toast to the young lovers" she said rather loudly.

I rolled my eyes "Thanks mum"

"Did you have a nice day today?" Abi asked dad.

"Oh, you know, any day away from work is a nice day" he smiled "Seeing Cat is the highlight of course" he winked at me "But the town is charming. We had a tour of the RSC this afternoon"

"Oh, nice. Did you see any of the rehearsals going on?" she asked.

"A little" mum said, taking over. "They were rehearsing for the evening performance of *The Constant Wife*. We got to express how much we enjoyed the play to one of the actors. It was lovely"

"Oh, that's nice. I'm sure they appreciated that" Abi smiled.

"What did you get up to?" mum asked "Anything exciting?"

"We went for lunch, and then to the butterfly farm"

"Oh, I do so love the butterfly farm. I insist on going every time we're here" mum smiled.

"I was lovely" Abi said "If not a little hot and humid"

This was going well. Very well. I relaxed, and enjoyed the rest of the evening.

We got back to the house just after ten, and my parents went straight to bed. I got a couple of beers from the fridge, and a blanket from my bedroom.

"Come" I said, taking Abi's hand.

I lead her out into the back garden, and put my two sun loungers next to each other.

"What are you doing?" Abi asked.

"Trust me. Come, lay back"

She got on the one next to me, and I covered us in the blanket.

"Close your eyes, recline fully back, and look up" I said.

She did as such, and I followed suit.
She gasped "Oh my God"
The night sky was dark and clear, and millions of stars sparkled above us.
"This is amazing"
It truly was an amazing sight.
"I lay here often, connecting the dots in my mind, drawing pretty pictures"
"It's beautiful"
We lay for a while, drinking our beers in silence, staring up at the night sky.
"Hey, it's late, I should go" she said, checking her watch.
"My God, it's almost midnight" I said, shocked.
"Or, can I sleep on your sofa?" she asked "It'll save me having to wait for a taxi to turn up"
I knew what she meant; there was nobody else there, and she didn't like being alone.
"You can stay" I smiled.
"Oh, great, thanks"
"But not on the sofa"
"Oh, you have another spare room?" She asked.
"No"
"You mean?"
"Yes"
"Are you sure?"
"Look, just because we sleep together, doesn't mean we have to have sex right?"
She laughed "Of course not"
"Good. We can *sleep* together"
"I'd like that"
I took her hand "Come on then"

After we had removed makeup, brushed teeth, etc. we lay in bed in the dark.

I was petrified. Is this what normal women do? Sure. Why not? It's ok to actually sleep in the same bed isn't it?

We lay in silence for a while, and I got more and more anxious with each passing second.

And then...

I felt a cautious hand seek out mine, and hold on to it. She squeezed it gently, reassuring me that it was ok to be nervous.

I took a deep breath, and relaxed.

I slept better that night than I ever had before.

23. Wallflower Blossom.

The following morning, I woke totally refreshed, and in a good place mentally.
But then I turned my head and saw empty space and panicked instantly. Had it been a dream? Where was she? Had she left in the middle of the night? Oh God, what had I done now?
The bedroom door opened, and she came in, holding two mugs of coffee.
Jesus Kate. I dropped back onto my pillow with relief. What the hell was wrong with me??
"You thought I'd gone" she smiled.
"Yes"
"I wouldn't do that" she said, putting the cups on the bedside table.
She got back into bed and hugged into me "I would never do that"
I didn't know whether to cry with joy or cry out of frustration. What was wrong with my mind?
"Coffee is getting cold" she smiled as we lay staring into each other's eyes.
I nodded.
We sat up, and she passed me a mug.
"Thank you"
"You're welcome. Thank you for letting me stay"
"You're welcome" I smiled.
"How are we going to explain this away to your mother? She'll likely think we enjoyed a night of hot, steamy, passionate love making"

"Ugh, God, don't. She'll be insufferable"
She laughed, almost spilling her coffee.
"Are they up?"
"If they are, they've gone out"
I checked the time; it was almost nine.
"Probably. Dad has gone for a run, and mum for a long walk. It is what they do on Sunday mornings. She'll come back with the papers, and they'll sit and read them for a few hours, drinking tea, and eating croissants"
"Very proper" she giggled.
"Yeah, they have their ways" I said "Bless them"
"You want to shower first?" I asked.
"Sure. You stay here, finish your coffee"
She kissed me and went off to the bathroom.
I lay in silence, clutching my mug and smiling. This was how I wanted to wake up every day. Without the nervous paranoia of course. And without my parents being here. But, with her.
Definitely with her.

After showering and dressing, we sat out in the garden with toast and orange juice. Dad was in the shower, and mum hadn't returned yet.
The sun shone down gently upon us, that early morning sunshine that warms your soul.
It was blissful.
Until mum came home.
"Oh, morning Abigail" she said, walking out into the garden.
"Morning Mrs Harrington"
Mum had a stupid grin on her face. This wasn't good.

"Morning mother"
"Morning dear" she smiled. "Abi stayed over?"
"It would appear so" I said.
"I see" she smiled. "I got croissants"
"I've just had toast. Abi?"
"No thank you" she smiled.
"Well, I'll go make a pot of tea for your father and I"
She leaned in and kissed my cheek "You look happy"
I swear I saw a tear in her eye as she walked off to the kitchen.
"That wasn't so bad" Abi said "I was expecting worse"
"So was I" I said, equally as surprised at mum's restraint. And the show of emotion. If I had doubted it before, I suspected that in that brief moment in time, my mother loved me. In whatever way she was capable of doing.

Mum and dad left to go home at midday, leaving a very quiet house behind them. I was relieved and sad at the same time. I would miss dad without question. But mum? I still wasn't sure of her sincerity.
"What do we do now?" Abi asked.
"I have an idea. Is Mark home?"
"Should be. What are you thinking?"
"I have so much food. My parents bought half of Waitrose. Can you take what you want? Please?"
She laughed. "I'm sure that can be arranged. Are you sure?"
"It'll all go to waste"
"Ok" she picked up her phone and text Mark.
He responded almost immediately, asking for the address.

"He's on his way"
"Good" I smiled. "Do you mind?"
"Of course not, why would I mind if you don't want to be alone with me?"
"What?" my face dropped.
"I'm kidding" she smiled "It'll be fun to have Mark around"
"Thank God for that"
"Sorry, I didn't mean to mess with your head"
"No, it's fine. I'm twenty seven; I should be able to handle a joke"
"And can you?" she asked, furtively.
"Yes"
Ten minutes later, the gay tornado hit my little home.
"Ladies" he smiled "Looking absolutely fab today"
"As are you my dear" Abi said, kissing his cheek.
He came in, fully made up, and dressed to kill.
"I'll ask you about your weekend in a moment, but for a second… it's all about me" he beamed.
"How was the concert?" I asked.
"Oh, since you asked. Divine! Abba tribute, I danced into the small hours. It was perfect"
"Sounds amazing" I said.
"You should come to one" he suggested "You'll love it"
"Oh I'm sure I would" I said. "Right up my street"
"You're getting there little wallflower" he smiled.
"Soon you'll be spreading your blossom around all over the place"
"That's a lovely thing to say" I said and hugged him
"Thank you"
"Welcome darling. Now where's all the free food? That's the real reason I'm here"

"Oh, you cheeky sod" I chuckled.

24. Tragedy Behind a Mask.

We spent an amazing afternoon with Mark, and they left with his little Corsa packed full of food.
After they had gone, I closed the front door and sat on the doormat. I was mentally exhausted. But, I knew I had a house to clean.
I took a breath, got up, put some music on, and got to work.
Cleaning was good for my mind, as it focussed me on a specific task, giving me no time to drift into depression. Three hours later, the place looked like a show home once more.
I sat on the sofa with a loud sigh. I felt good. The last few days had given me a glimpse of what life could be like. I was grateful for that at least.
As it was almost eight o'clock, I had a quick shower and washed my hair ready for the morning.
It was too late for dinner, so I just sat on the sofa with some yoghurt and fruit. The weekend had been good. Enjoyable. It that what normal people did with their free time? I guessed so. My life would be different from now on. I would spend my weekends with Abi. Wouldn't I? Would she want to? What if she didn't? What if she hadn't really enjoyed our time together? Should we have had sex? Would that make her happy? Would it make me happy? No. It wouldn't. I don't know why, but at the moment, it just wouldn't.
Why not? What was wrong with me? Surely it's what normal people do in a relationship? Abi was normal.

Why wasn't I?
I felt instantly profoundly sad, and started crying.
"Why am I not normal?" I sobbed aloud.
I had once again fallen into my mind's self-pity trap.
Shit. I stood and walked to the mirror in the bathroom.
I stared at myself in the mirror. My eyes were red and puffy from the tears. My hair was too short. My...
No. Stop. Stop it with the negativity. What are the positives? There must be some. Right?
I stared.
I had good skin. I liked the natural colour of my hair. My eyes were a lovely blue-grey.
I stepped back and looked down at myself. I was slim. Not stupid diet-driven skinny, just slim. Nice legs, toned by cycling and running. Boobs. Hmm. Could do with being a bit bigger. However, that meant they were firm and not drooping. Thankfully.
Compare the positive to the negative. Body wise? Just my hair length. The rest, I am happy with.
So, what is the *real* problem? My mind? How do I solve that? I could speak to mum's friend, as she suggested. Alternatively, I could think about it myself.
What was the cause? Sean's death?
Most likely, as I was fine before that.
So how do I get over that?
Do I just carry on as I am? As the she chameleon? Hiding behind a mask?
My mind is drawn to negative thoughts, like a moth to a flame. How do I stop that from happening?
I could message Abi. Let her know what was going on in my head and let her be the voice of reason.
Is that fair? She *had* suggested it though...

But I didn't want to be a dead weight around her neck.
I picked up my phone, and typed: How do I stop feeling guilty about Sean's death?
I hit Send and hoped for the best.
Typing...
Then, the message came through.
Speak to his mother. If you need forgiveness or absolution, that is where you'll find it.
Oh my God. Why hadn't I thought of that?
It's so simple.
Sean's mum lived in Market Harborough, I had her address in my little address book. How would I get there? By train. Or, maybe...
I text back: Thanks mum. X.
Then I text Abi: You think Mark would drive us up to Market Harborough this weekend? I could pay him.
A minute or so later, I got a message saying I had been added to the group *Roadtrip*.
A message came up from an unknown number:
If you have petrol money, I'll take you anywhere my lovely.
Had to be Mark.
Thank you dearest, I really appreciate it. I need to speak to Sean's mum.
Who's Sean?
Ask Abi. I need her to forgive me.
Sounds serious. It's not a problem, happy to drive.
Thanks darling.

I got a call from Abi a few minutes later.
"Hey, what's going on? You ok? Mark was asking about Sean"

"I think I figured out what I need to do in order to move on"
"Speak to his mum?"
"Yes. I need to hear her say it wasn't my fault"
"You're seeking absolution?"
"I think it'll help"
"You think she blames you?"
"What? No, not at all"
"You sure it's wise, dragging up the bad memories? Will she want to do that, just for your sake?"
"I'll speak to her before we go"
"Ok, if you're sure"
"Abi, I'm tired of being how I am. It's exhausting, and I fear it'll lead to something bad eventually"
"Hey, don't be talking like that" she snapped.
"I've never thought about it, I just fear it'll escalate and end up there eventually"
"If you ever think like that, or it just pops into your mind, you call me. You hear?"
"It'll never come to that. Not if I speak to her"
"Hmmm" she sounded unconvinced.
"Look Abi, I'm sorry I mentioned it. I just read so many stories about depressed people…"
"Ok stop there" she said before I could finish "I get it. We'll go up. You speak to her and make this better"
"That's the plan"
"Ok. See you tomorrow"
"Look forward to it"

It was time to rid myself of this mask. I just needed to speak to Sean's mum to make sure it was ok to come up and see her.

25. Absolution in the Absence of Sin.

Sean's mum had been absolutely lovely when I spoke to her on the phone. She had been so happy to hear from me that it brought on yet something else: guilt. Guilt for not having called her before. However, that was guilt for another time. Right now, I had a problem; she wouldn't be home this weekend. Instead, she had suggested coming up this evening.
It was feasible of course, as it was only about an hour away, but I needed to check if my Roadtrip Group were available.
I checked my watch; eleven. An hour to go. I was meeting Abi and Mark for lunch, and would ask them then.
Nerves set in. I really needed this.

I walked out into the sunlight, and found my friends sitting on the steps.
"Hey guys" I said, sitting next to them.
"Hey" Abi said, taking my hand "You ok?"
"I'm good. Shall we?"
"Yes please, I'm starving" Mark said.
I waited patiently for them to order before asking.
"Erm, can I ask a favour?" I said to Mark.
"Of course you can gorgeous" he smiled.
"The trip this weekend. Can we do it this evening instead?"
"This evening? Why?" he sounded disappointed.

"Sean's mum isn't home this weekend" I said.
"Oh, no" he said, still sounding disappointed.
"I'll make it up to you" I offered.
"How?"
"How about we go somewhere overnight? My treat?"
He raised an eyebrow "You'd pay for a hotel?"
"Yes" I smiled "For all three of us"
"Deal" he smiled.
I looked at Abi.
"Deal" she said.
"Oh, thank God"
"We'll pick you up at five"
"I'll get McDonalds or something for dinner" I said
"Whatever you want"
"Sounds good to me" he smiled.
That was a huge relief, and a huge weight off my mind. We sat and had lunch in the sun, chatting excitedly about where we could go for our overnight adventure.

The rest of the afternoon passed by fairly uneventfully. The team were still just "keeping busy". The drafts for the web designs would be in by the end of the week, so I didn't really mind.
I left at half past four, and had a quick shower and change. I wanted to look nice for Shaun's mum, but not over the top. I wore my green wrap round dress and converse. It looked nice, but not overly formal. Perfect.
I had butterflies in my stomach. Even though she had sounded lovely over the phone, seeing her face-to-face was different. She could look into my eyes. What if she was different? Would I be able to cope? Shit.

A beep from outside shook me from my bad thoughts. Shit, they were here.
Mark's car was parked out on the road, and he was waving frantically.
I waved back, grabbed my bag, and ran out to the car. We got a McDonalds before hitting the main road, and were on our way.

The drive took just under two hours in the end, as we'd hit peak traffic. Fortunately, the mood in the car remained positive, and we arrived in good spirits.
"We'll go for a walk" Abi said as we stood outside the house. "You just let us know when you're finished"
"Ok"
"Good luck" she kissed my cheek.
"Good look gorgeous, hope it goes ok" Mark said.
I took a deep breath and walked up the path to the front door.

The door opened before I could knock, and Sean's mum took me in her arms.
"My God Kathrina, it's so good to see you" she said, crying "It's been so long"
"I'm really sorry. I should have come sooner"
"It's ok, I understand. Come on in"
We went inside, and walked into the kitchen.
"I made tea if you'd like some?"
"Yes please"
We sat at the table and she poured tea.
I thanked her, and held out my hand to pick up the mug; it was trembling badly.

She took hold of my hand. "It's difficult. It has been difficult for a long time. I understand" she said kindly.
Tears ran down my cheeks.
"I'm so sorry" I said.
"It's fine Katie dear, I know how difficult it has been for you"
"It's been so hard" I said "Living with the guilt"
"Guilt?" She looked puzzled "Guilt for what?"
"I should have been with him. I was on my period and wasn't feeling well, so didn't go to the party. If I had been there he'd still be here"
She fixed me with a stern look.
Oh shit. She's angry.
But, to my surprise, she didn't shout at me.
Instead, she spoke calmly, but sternly.
"Now you look here young lady" she said, holding my hands "That's complete nonsense, you hear? You can't think like that"
"But..."
"But nothing. Hindsight is a wonderful thing Kathrina. You were ill. Blaming yourself is nonsense"
It was silent for a moment.
"My God" she said eventually "Have you been blaming yourself this whole time?"
I nodded.
"That's crazy. God alone knows what it's done to your mind. What is it you need from me?"
"I need forgiveness"
"Forgiveness? For something that wasn't your fault?"
Our eyes met, tears running down my face.
She held my hands "Why..."
"I really need this" I said, cutting her off.

"It's been so hard, and I'm a mess. My life has been shit since he left. I need this to try make it better. And I know that sounds terribly selfish and awful. And I can't even imagine what you have been through. Oh God, I'm so selfish. I'm sorry, I shouldn't have come…"

"I forgive you" she said, looking deep into my soul.

"What?"

"I forgive you"

I was stunned. "You do?"

"Of course I do. Why wouldn't I? Though to be honest, I don't know what I'm forgiving you for. But, if it's my forgiveness you need, you have it. It's time to move on Kate, Sean is gone. He's been gone for a long time. Holding on to his ghost isn't good for you. It almost destroyed me, but I learned to cope with my loss. It still hurts, but it doesn't rule my life anymore. You understand what I'm saying?"

Her kindly face looked at me, and I burst into tears.

"I miss him so much"

"Come here" she said, rising from her chair.

I got up and she hugged me tight, stroking my hair. This is what I had needed from my mother. This is what she should have done. Years of grief and anguish flooded out, and I cried like I'd never cried before.

I sat quietly in the back of the car on the way home. Sean's mum had made me promise to come back and see her soon. I stared out into the gathering darkness. Had that been it? I had the absolution I had sought. Her words about moving on made sense too, if she could do it, I should be able to. It was everything I had wanted to hear.

But still, I didn't feel any better. Was this normal? Would it come with time?

Or, was there something else? Something as yet unresolved. I had no idea. I only knew that I didn't feel any different than I had before speaking to Sean's mum.

I felt relieved and angry at the same time. Relieved that I had been forgiven by Sean's mum. And an intense anger. For my own mum.

She should have been there for me like Sean's mum had just been. She should have held me, stroked my hair, told me it was going to be ok.

I knew this already, but it had really been driven home to me just ten minutes ago.

I needed to speak to mum, to confront her directly.

I knew I had already shouted at her, but that had been over the phone.

I needed to see her eyes when she told me she was sorry.

She had offered to speak to me as a mum and psychologist. Maybe this was the right time to accept the offer.

Or was it? I didn't know. Maybe I should talk to Abi about it.

My travel companions left me to my thoughts in the back, trying hard not to disturb me during the drive home.

Not a single word had been spoken when Mark pulled up outside my home.

Abi turned to face me "Are you going to be ok?"

"I'll be fine" I lied.

"You sure? I can stay?"

I shook my head "You'll need to get ready for work in the morning. I'll be fine. Thank you though"
"You just let us know if you need us my love" Mark said.
"I will" I said putting my hand on his shoulder "Thank you for doing this"
"Any time" he smiled.
I got out, and Abi walked me to the door.
"Are you sure?" she asked again.
"How will you get ready for work?"
"I'll get up earlier and go home first"
"Are you sure?"
"Of course" she smiled, and ran over to the car.
Seconds later, it drove off, leaving us alone in the dark.
"Let's go to bed" she smiled.
I opened the door, and we went straight to bed.
She held me all night, sensing my needs perfectly.
I was in love with this woman, I thought.
Is this what normal women feel?

26. A Clash of Emotions.

For the rest of that week, I was as close to being a normal woman as I thought I'd ever get. We had received the web designs and had gone through them for two days before settling on our final choice.
I would be fantastic. I had met up with Abi and Mark for lunch each day so far, and it had been good for my soul. But, today was Thursday. I was taking half a day off to go visit my mother. It was time.

I caught the midday train to Oxford, and walked from the station to their house. Dad's car was gone.
A regret. I had really wanted to see him, more so than my mother.
I knocked, and my mother opened the door.
"Kathrina" she smiled "Come"
She stood aside and let me in. She closed the door and took me through to the kitchen.
Would you like some tea of coffee?"
"Tea please"
"I have a pot made" she smiled.
We sat at the table, and she poured.
"How did it go with Shaun's mother?" she asked.
I wanted to slap her for even uttering his name, but restrained myself.
"It went ok, though nothing changed"
"Nothing?" she said, raising an eyebrow. This, she hadn't expected. She'd expected me to say that my world changed as she spoke her words of forgiveness. But it hadn't.

"No. Although, it made me realise something"
"What?"
"As I broke down in grief, she held me, stroked my hair, and told me it was all going to be ok. After, in the car home I thought to myself; that should have been you. You should have been the one to hold me, comfort me. But, as always, you were nowhere to be seen"
"I thought we went through this already?" she said nervously.
"Oh, I thought the same. But then, I reasoned that doing it over the phone is cheating. I can't see whether you're being sincere or not. I need to look into your eyes when you speak the words"
"What words?"
"You're going to tell me how incredibly sorry you are that you weren't there for me"
"I am?"
"Yes mother, you are"
I sat back, and folded my arms.
"What? Now? Here?"
"Why not?"
She looked nervous.
"Go on" I said.
"No, I…"
"Go on!" I shouted.
She was shocked into silence, and just stared at me.
"Kathrina, please" she managed eventually.
I stared into her cold eyes, daring her to say the words.
"I'm sorry" she said.
"And?"
"And? I'm sorry. What more do you want?"

"That's it? That's all you have to say? For almost five years, my life has been pure hell. I hate myself, I can't bear to be around other people. I'm completely broken, and you did nothing"
I could feel myself welling up "I'm scared of my own bloody shadow! And all you can say is sorry?" I shouted. "You did nothing!"
"That's not true!" she said angrily.
I laughed "You've lied about it so much that the lie becomes reality" I said, laughing. "I came here for your love, because my mother is supposed to love me isn't she?"
"I do love you!" she spat.
"Oh behave mother! You love the *idea* of me. You loved me before I broke. Before I left home, before I cut off my precious hair. You loved *her*, not *me*" I said, pounding my chest. "All I ever wanted was your love, to have you hold me. But you couldn't bring yourself to do it because I'd become a bloody disappointment"
"That's not true Kathrina"
"Oh, spare me. I can see it in your eyes. They're as cold as a bloody snakes"
"You should never have left home!" she shouted "You should have just stayed here and gone to Oxford. Then you would still be my beautiful princess"
"Ha!" I exclaimed "And there it is! The truth is out!"
"Kathrina…" she said, but I cut her off.
"Enough!" I shouted, then calmed myself "Enough. I think we're done here" I got up, picked up my bag, and left her crying at the kitchen table.
I thought I would break down in tears as I walked the streets towards the station, but I didn't.

I felt absolutely nothing. Empty. Emotionless. All that was left was resolve. I knew what I needed now.

On the journey home, I text Abi, and asked if she could stay over tonight.

To my surprise, she agreed readily, and said she'd be round at about six, but that she'd have to leave early tomorrow as she had a meeting at half past eight.

I got home around ten past five, and headed straight for the shower. I washed my hair and did my legs.

I took the time to moisturise with my best Chanel moisturiser, and got dressed.

She arrived just after six o'clock, holding a Thai takeaway.

"Hope you don't mind?" she said as she set the bag on the table.

"No, I love Thai" I said.

We ate, watched tv, and talked about our day. I told her about my talk with mum, and she got pretty upset.

"Why didn't you call me after?"

"I just wanted to be alone for a while, I'm sorry. I'm not really that upset about it"

"You aren't?" she asked, puzzled.

"No, I had prepared myself for the confrontation. It wasn't as bad as I had thought" I lied. I hadn't prepared myself at all, and it had been far worse that I had anticipated. I just didn't want her to be upset.

"Are you sure you're ok?" she asked.

"Actually" I said "I'm not. But, there's something you can do to help"

"Oh?"

I looked deep into her eyes "I want you to make love to me. Make me feel something good"
"What? Are you sure?" she asked.
"I've never ben surer of anything in my life. I love you Abigail, and I'm ready"
She kissed me deeply "I love you too"
"Then take me to bed" I smiled.

And so, we went to bed. I had prepared myself for the physical act of sex, but it surpassed even my wildest imaginations. It was like she had said when we had first broached the subject; she made love. And she did. With a passion. I had never felt anything like it before, and doubted I ever would again. She was gentle, yet firm, loving, caring, fierce, and just incredibly good at it. I was lost in a whirlwind of ecstasy, desire, and passion for almost an hour.
After, we lay exhausted, breathing heavily.
"Oh my God" I said quietly, turning to face her "Is that how normal women feel?"
"What?" she asked, breathlessly.
"Never mind, thank you"
Her face was flushed, as was my own.
"You're welcome" she said. "Are you ok?"
"I've never been better" I smiled. That was not a lie; I had never felt better than I did in that moment. Nor would I ever be again.
"I love you" I said.
"I love you too"
I held her close and fell asleep in her arms.

27. Merry Christmas, Mr Lawrence.

I woke up to the sounds of birdsong through my open window. The sun filtered in through gaps in the curtains, giving an enticing glimpse of the beauty waiting beyond. The bed next to me was empty, and the mattress long cold. She had left very early.
I checked my phone; 07.05, Friday, 21 August. The weather was going to be nice all day.
I stretched, and got out of bed. The cat, which had been sleeping at the foot of the bed, jumped down and meowed sweetly. She wanted food.
"Come on Tab" I smiled.
She followed me out, and I overfilled her bowl.
"You're a lovely cat" I said, stroking her "Be good"
I had a tidy round, making sure everything was perfect, then had a shower. After, I dried and dressed my hair, applied my makeup, and chose my best underwear.
I took my time getting ready; I wanted to look my best today. I smiled at my reflection as I checked myself before heading out. It wasn't going to get any better than this. Perfect.
I left my lovely home behind, and walked into the town. There weren't many people around, as the tourist season was almost over now. Traffic was busy, as it always was during rush hour, but it didn't bother me today.
I walked to Marco's to get my usual coffee.
Above me, cirrus clouds feathered the sky.

It reminded me of Abi. Sweet Abi, keeper of my heart.
"Ah, bella signora Kate" Marco smiled as I walked in.
"Morning Marco"
"You look beautiful today, you have important meeting?"
"You could say that" I smiled.
"Ah, I knew. You sit, I make you coffee"
"You're a sweet man Marco"
He brought my coffee a few minutes later, together with the usual cannoli.
"You knock them dead" he smiled "Is that what they say?"
"Yes it is" I smiled. I kissed his cheek "Thank you Marco"
"You have good day signora Kate"
"You too Marco, and thank you"

I walked along the river, sipping my coffee. It really was a beautiful day, I was very grateful for that at least.
The geese swam over as soon as I came near the water's edge.
"Sorry geese, I have nothing" I smiled.
Unperturbed, they followed me as I walked along, until I finally lost sight of them behind a bush. I walked on towards the church. I wanted to see Mary today, it had been such a long time since I had last visited. I picked some late blooming flowers to make up for it.
The sun beams filtered through the trees, throwing spotlights on some of the headstones. But not Mary's. How very typical, I thought.
"Morning Mary" I said, stroking her headstone.
I knelt down and placed the flowers on her grave.

"I'm sorry Mary. It's been such a long time, and I really wish I could sit and chat. But, I have an appointment. I'll see you soon though"
I walked out of the graveyard and headed towards the river. I could hear the water rushing over the weir as I approached. A lone Heron sat at the bottom of the rushing water, waiting patiently for a fish to fly past. It really was a beautiful day.
Just up ahead, I heard the rushing traffic on the main road. It was busy and noisy.
The noise increased in volume as I got nearer, and I put my earphones in to deaden the sound. The beautiful tones of Ryuichi Sakamoto's Merry Christmas Mr Lawrence filled my senses. Its beauty calming my nerves. That's better, I thought. I can concentrate now. I walked up to the bridge that crossed the river.
The path on the other side headed back towards the town and the life I knew.
However, I wasn't going that way today. I placed my coffee and cannoli on the handrail. Cars rushed past in a muted form of madness. Up ahead, I saw it coming. I moved forward and closed my eyes in readiness.
"Oh Sean" I said, and stepped off the edge into the space beyond.

28. Abigail's Nightmare.

I woke just before six, earlier than I had wanted to. Or had needed to. But, it was light outside, so I thought I may as well get up and go home to get ready for work.
Kate was asleep next to me. I stared at her for a while. We had made love.
It had been fantastic. I hadn't experienced anything like it before. The temptation to reach out and take her in my arms was great. However, I resisted. There would be time for that later, we had our whole lives to look forward to. Together.
I smiled, and carefully got out of bed and gathered my clothes off the floor. I gave her one last look, then closed the bedroom door.
The house was pristine. We were so alike in many ways.
I dressed, and quietly closed the front door as I left. There was a bit of a chill in the air as I walked home, the roads were empty, as was the town. The geese and swans were still sleeping. It was like a ghost town. I liked it.

When I got home, I had a shower and got ready for work. I was sitting in the kitchen making breakfast just seven. Still too early to go to work.
Mark joined me a few minutes later.
"Morning sweetheart" he said groggily.
"Morning my lovely" I smiled.

He walked to the fridge to get his usual glass of orange juice, then stopped. He thought for a moment, then turned to me "Were you out all night you slapper?"
"Yes" I grinned.
"Oh my God, really?" he said.
I nodded.
"Good for you. How was it?"
"It was spectacular"
"That's good" he smiled "How was it for her?"
My smile disappeared. I hadn't thought about that. How had it been for her? She seemed to enjoy it, but something hadn't seemed quite right. Easy to see now, but at the time I had been caught up in the heat of our lovemaking.
"I... I don't know"
He frowned "You don't know? Did she enjoy it?"
"I think so"
Something... I struggled to think. Something wasn't right. Something she had said. I hadn't quite caught it. Something like: *Is that how normal women feel.*
What an odd thing to say.
"Hello?" he snapped his fingers in my face.
"Oh, sorry. Listen, she said something"
"What?"
"She said, *is that how normal women feel?*"
He pulled a face "What an odd thing to say"
"And she told me she loved me"
"Aw, that's so sweet" he said, clutching his chest.
"No. I mean, yes it is, but we had agreed it was too early for that. We had agreed to take it slow, to date, to get to know each other better. Until then we were just fond of each other"

"That's weird"
I dropped my toast. "Oh no"
"What is it?"
"Shit. We need to get over there"
"What? Why?"
"We need to get over there, now!" I shouted.
He ran off to his bedroom and dressed in a hurry.
"This better be important" he said, meaning important enough for him to go out without makeup.
"It's important. Quick!"
We raced downstairs and drove over to Kate's house.

Traffic had increased significantly since I walked home, and it took us almost twenty minutes to get there.
I ran up to the front door and knocked. And knocked.
"Come on Kate"
There was no response. Shit. I tried the door; it was open.
"Kate?" I called. No answer. Shit. I ran to the bedroom, but it was empty. The bed had been made, and it was spotless.
"Kate?" I checked all the rooms, but she wasn't there. She wasn't home. The cat purred at my feet "Hey Tabby, where's Kate?" She didn't answer of course.
I walked into the kitchen, where something caught my eye.
Carefully arranged on the kitchen table were five envelopes. One of them had my name on it, the rest were for Mark, Mother, Dad, and James.
"Oh no Kate" I said.
With shaking hands, I picked up the envelope bearing my name and opened it. It smelled of Coco Chanel.

Tears were already streaming down my face as I unfolded the note.
It was written in her beautiful handwriting, and I knew what it was going to be before I read it. Oh no, Kate.

My beautiful Abigail,

I want to thank you for making my life so beautifully wonderful over the last few months. You were the first person I think I ever loved, and the only person I ever made love to. For that, I thank you.
I told you when I first met you that I could feel alone, even when I was with you. And I recall the conversation we had about what I should do if I ever feared the worst. I'm so sorry my love, I failed.
If there is anything that should bring you comfort, it is that I am at peace now. No more pain. No more negativity. No more masks. I'm finally free.
Don't think badly of me my love, I can do that enough for both of us. Remember me fondly, and with love.
Look around you, this home I created is yours now. I left it to you. I won't blame you if you sell it, so don't worry about that. It's what normal women would do.

Think of me when you see cirrus clouds above.

I love you, and only you.

Kathrina. X.

"Oh Kate" I said "What have you done?"
I ran outside, in floods of tears.

"Mark, Mark!" I shouted. He scrambled out of the car and ran over "What's wrong?"
"She's gone" I cried.
"To work?"
I shook my head.
"Where is she?"
"We need to find her Mark"
"She's not here?"
"No, she's gone somewhere"
"Where?"
Good question. Where the hell had she gone? Think. Where would she go? Where?
Where would she go on her last day on earth? Where?
"Mary" I said.
"Mary?"
"Holy Trinity. We need to get there now!"
We ran to the car, and set off. We made it as far as the end of the road before hitting traffic.
"Jesus. Pull over, we'll have to run" I said.
He pulled over, and he started running towards the bridge.
"It'll be quicker to go the other way" I shouted "By the weir"
We ran through the park, and headed towards the weir. Mark was lagging behind, his lack of fitness showing. I left him and ran on. I had to find her.
Wait, was that her on the bridge?
I shouted "Kate!" but she seemed not to hear. I made the bottom of the bridge and ran onto it. She had just placed her coffee on the railing and turned to face the road. "Kate! No! No, no, no, no!" I shouted as I ran, but she didn't hear.

She turned her head and closed her eyes.

"No!" I was almost there.

I heard her say "Oh Sean", and she stepped forward.

"No, no, no, no!" I shouted" I grabbed hold of her dress just as she did so, and pulled her back.

She shouted out in surprise, and fell backwards, on top of me.

"No!" she shouted "No!"

She struggled, trying to break fee, but I put my arms around her and held on tight. She elbowed me in the ribs repeatedly, but I held on, regardless of the searing pain.

"What are you doing!" she shouted "Let me go!"

"Kate! Stop!" I said, but she didn't hear; she had earphones in.

I rolled her over so I was on top of her and pulled out one of her earphones "Kate!"

She opened her eyes, and stopped struggling immediately. "Abi?"

"What the hell are you doing Kate?"

"Abi, no. You're not supposed to be here" she said.

I slapped her hard, hard enough to make my palm sting.

"You promised me!" I shouted "You promised you'd tell me!" I went to slap her again, but the look of horror on her face made me stop.

"Abi…"

"Why would you do this? Why would you leave me behind? Why?" I cried.

"Sean" she said.

"Sean? Sean is dead Kate! He's dead. Gone! You're supposed to be here for me now!"

I looked down at her. Her cheek was bright red from where I had slapped her. I felt instantly bad.

"Kate..."

"What are you doing here Abi? This isn't how it was supposed to happen"

I pulled her to her feet, she looked beautiful. She was fully made up, and was wearing what were likely her best, or favourite clothes.

"What am I doing here? Are you mad? What the hell is this?" I asked, pulling out her note.

"Abi..."

"You promised me Kate. You promised"

"You have no idea what it's like" she cried.

"That's where you're wrong" I said. "Come on"

I dragged her along, away from any danger. We walked down into the park and sat on a bench. I was weary of any source of danger, so kept a close eye on her.

I didn't want her jumping up and sprinting into the weir.

Mark was walking towards us, having caught up.

"Abi!" he ran over. "Jesus, what is going on here?" he asked. He looked at Kate, then at me.

"Why don't you tell him Kate?" I said.

"You shouldn't be here" she said "You shouldn't be here"

"What?" he asked "Why are you all dressed up?"

I handed him the note. He read it.

"Oh Jesus, what the hell?" he said "Kate!"

"There's one for you too" I said "On her kitchen table"

"There is?" he seemed impressed.

"Mark!" I said.

"Sorry" he knelt down in front of Kate and took her hand "It's going to be ok sweetheart"
Shit. I remembered what she had said about her mother.
I took her in my arms. She resisted at first, but gave in eventually. I held her tight, and stroked her hair.
"It's going to be ok my love" I said "It's going to be ok"
"What do we do?" Mark asked, panicking "Hospital?"
"What for? She's not injured" I said.
"Oh, shit. What do we do?"
"Mark" I said calmly "Go to work. I've got this"
"Work? Shit" he checked his watch. "I'll be late"
"No" I said "Just go there now"
"But I'm not dressed"
"Mark, one day. Just do it. Go see Niamh, she'll sort you out"
"But what about you two?"
"We're going to be fine" I smiled "Go"
He kissed Kate's hand, and walked off towards the bridge. It would kill him to go into work without makeup, but he could get Niamh to sort him out.
I sat on the bench with Kate for about twenty minutes, just holding her and stroking her hair.
"We should go" I said eventually.
"I can't" she said.
I cupped her face with my hands "Look at me, look at me"
Reluctantly, she looked into my eyes. What I saw shocked me; there was nothing there. Kate had gone. Or was she just hiding behind yet another mask?
"We're going home"
"Abi..."

"We're going home" I insisted.
"We're going to get up, hold hands, and walk home. If you try to do anything, I swear to God…"
"I won't"
"Good. Come on" I stood and helped her up.
I pulled my phone from my pocket, and dialled my manager's number.
"John, its Abi. Look, I need a personal day. Yeah, I know. I'm sorry, I'll sort it from home, I have my laptop. I just need the day. Ok, thanks"
I dialled off, and handed my phone to Kate.
"Call whomever you need to call"
She took the phone and punched in a number.
I took the phone from her.
"What are you doing?" she asked.
"I'll sort it" A young sounding girl answered the phone.
"Hello?"
"Hi, is that Kate's office?" I asked.
"Yes, I'm her assistant Jenny, can I help?"
"Jenny, its Abigail, Kate's friend. Look, she's not well today, are you able to cover for her?"
"Oh no, is she ok?"
"She just needs a personal day"
"Oh, ok. Yes, well of course, I'll cover"
"Thank you Jenny, you're a star"
"Please give her my best wishes"
"I will, thank you Jenny"
I put my phone in my pocket "There. Done. Now we have all day to sort this mess out"
She didn't speak, in fact, she didn't speak all the way home. To our home. I had decided; I was moving in. She needed help.

29. Actions, Consequences.

I felt a mixture of anger and love towards her.
This was not how it was supposed to have happened. It wasn't.
I was supposed to be in the loving arms of my Sean by now. Away from this madness. Away from my madness.
And I was just that; mad. I would be committed. I was a suicide risk. I'd be taken away, and locked up somewhere where I'd be pumped full of drugs to keep me sedated.
I looked over to my left. The weir. I could break free, and run. No. It was too late now. I had missed my opportunity.
How the hell had she found me? It wasn't supposed to have happened this way.
She was supposed to have gone to work, and grown concerned because I wasn't in or answering messages. Then she'd eventually go to the house and find the note. Or, maybe she would have seen it on the news. Or something. Anything other than this. I was supposed to be in my Sean's arms. Why was she here?
We made it back to the bungalow, and I smiled involuntarily. I thought I'd never see it again. Tab was on the path, rolling around in the morning sun.
"Tab" I said, crying. Abi let me go and I picked up my beautiful cat.
"Oh Tab" I said, holding her tight. She purred and licked my hand.

Abi opened the door "Come on" she said "Let's go in" We went inside, and she lead me straight out into the back garden.

"Sit"

I sat.

"Can I trust you?" she asked. "I'm going to make some tea. Can I trust you?"

"What? Yes, of course"

She knelt in front of me, and looked into my eyes. Whatever she saw seemed to satisfy her. "Ok"

She got up, and went inside to the kitchen.

I stared down at the ground. What the hell had happened? It had all gone to plan. It had all been perfect. Until Abi had shown up.

I didn't have time to ponder it further, as she came out holding the envelopes and a box of matches.

"We won't be needing these" she said, tearing them up, and then setting fire to them.

My beautiful words, going up in smoke. Well, beautiful, except for my mother's note. That one was definitely not beautiful.

She went back inside, and emerged a minute or so later with two mugs of tea. She handed one to me, and pulled over a chair so she was sitting directly opposite me.

She didn't speak. She just sipped her tea and stared. The silence was suffocating.

"How?" I asked eventually.

"How what?" she asked.

"How did you know?"

"Where you were, or that you were going to kill yourself"

I winced. The words cut like a knife; kill yourself.
I hadn't thought of it in that sense. To me, I was setting myself free.

"Both"

"Well" she said, and took another sip of tea. "I was sat in my little kitchen, eating my toast when it came to me. Mark asked me if I'd been out all night, and I told him I had. He worked out that we'd "Done it", and asked how it had been. I told him it had been spectacular"

"Spectacular?" I asked.

She nodded "Spectacular. Anyway. Then he asked me how I thought it had been for you. That knocked me for six. I hadn't even considered that. But, then I started thinking about it, remembering little things. You asked *Is this how normal women feel*? Or something like that. It struck me as odd. Why would you say that? It was then that I knew"

"You knew from me saying that?"

"No, not from that. From that, I realised that you're not gay. You aren't. In the slightest"

She looked at me, waiting for me to say otherwise, but I didn't. She was right.

"Thanks for confirming" she said, her voice trembling, despite her angry confidence.

I had just broken her heart.

She gathered herself, and continued "Anyway, after that, you told me you loved me. That's when I knew. It just didn't register at the time"

I looked puzzled. "How?"

"We promised we'd take it slow Kate, go out on dates, get to know each other better. Remember that?"

"Of course"
"We were fond of each other, remember that too? We weren't going to talk about love until we knew"
"I knew" I said, defiantly. Of course I did.
She shook her head. "What you felt wasn't real. You knew you were going to kill yourself, so you said it because you knew you'd never get the chance to utter the words again"
That hit hard. She was right. Oh my God.
"How did I know where you were?" she asked, before I could object. "I didn't really. I reasoned you'd probably want to say goodbye to Mary before... Well, you know, killing yourself. That's where I was going. To the graveyard. But then I saw you on the bridge"
"I see" I said, not knowing what else to say.
"You see? You see? Is that it? For God's sake Kate. Talk to me"
"What am I supposed to say?" I asked. I regretted it instantly.
"Are you kidding? How about "I'm sorry Abi" or something"
"I'm sorry Abi" I said.
"Look at me, and say it again"
I stared into her eyes "I..."
I couldn't say it. I'd be lying. I wasn't sorry. I could see it in her eyes; she knew, and was angry. This is exactly what my mother would have seen in my eyes yesterday. Shit.
"You can't because you're not" she said evenly "And I'm ok with that"
This wasn't good. She should be furious, not ok.
"How long?" she asked.

"Pardon?"

"How long have you been planning this? When did you decide you were going to kill yourself?"

"Why?"

"Why? Oh, I don't know Kate, just humour me ok?" she said angrily. She took a breath, composed herself, and said "Just tell me"

"On the train to Oxford"

"To see your mother?"

"Yes"

"You decided you were going to throw away our life together, and just leave me behind to pick up the pieces, whilst sitting on the train?"

"Partially. The talk with my mother sealed it"

"Ok. So let me get this straight. You were on the train, thinking about killing yourself. You didn't bother calling me, like we agreed. Fine. I can at least pretend to understand that bit. But then, you had an argument with your mother, and *that* made up your mind?"

"Yes"

She shook her head. And laughed.

"Why are you laughing?" I asked. Why the hell was she laughing? This wasn't funny! This was my life!

"You were going to kill yourself to spite your mother" she said.

"What? No. I was going to be with Sean"

"Oh, spare me Kate. You were going to do it to make your mother feel bad"

"No, that's not true"

"You loved Sean?" she asked.

"What? Of course I did"

"And he loved you"

"Yes, why…?"
I wasn't sure where she was going with this, but I didn't like it. I didn't like her talking about Sean. Not like this.
"You think this is what he would have wanted? Hmm? You've been broken for so many years, hanging on to a ghost. Then you find me, and we're good together. We're *good* together Kate. You think he would want you to throw that away? Your chance of happiness? How stupid are you?"
"Pardon?" I said angrily.
"You heard. How stupid can you be? You think he's sat up there, looking down on you, seeing you happy for once, but still wanting you to kill yourself to be with him? You think he would want you to kill yourself? Would he?"
"I could have been with him" I said weakly.
"Bullshit. You know what happens after death Kate? Nothing. Zero. Nada. You cease to exist. That's it"
"That's not true"
"Oh behave. Of course it is. On the other hand, you know what happens to the people you leave behind?"
I looked down at the floor. I didn't want to hear this.
"You have any idea how I felt? Coming here, reading this?" she thrust the note into my hand. "Read it"
"I know what it says Abigail" I said angrily.
"Read it. Out loud"
"What? No"
"Read it" she insisted.
I unfolded the note. Oh, please, don't make me do this.
"Please Abi"
"Just read the bloody note Kate" she said angrily.

Tears welled up in my eyes as I started reading.
"My beautiful Abigail, I want to thank you for making my life so beautifully wonderful over the last few months. You were the first person I think I ever loved, and the only person I ever made love to.
For that, I thank you" I paused. I didn't want to go on.
"Keep going" she said.
"I told you when I first met you that I could feel alone, even when I was with you. And I recall the conversation we had about what I should do if I ever feared the worst. I'm so sorry my love, I failed.
If there is anything that should bring you comfort, it is that I am at peace now. No more pain. No more negativity. No more masks. I'm finally free.
Don't think badly of me my love, I can do that enough for both of us. Remember me fondly, and with love.
Look around you, this home I created is yours now.
I left it to you. I won't blame you if you sell it, so don't worry about that. It's what normal women would do.
Think of me when you see cirrus clouds above.
I love you, and only you"
By the time I'd finished reading, tears were streaming down my face.
"Do you mean any of that?" she asked, evenly. Coldly even.
That shocked me. "What?"
"Do you mean any of that? Any of it? At all?"
"Of course I do"
She snatched the note from my hand, scrunched it up, and threw it away. "That's what I think of that" she said angrily.

"What are you doing?" I said, scrambling after the scrunched up paper.
I picked it up, and clutched it to my heart.
"See?" she said "*Now* I know. But just then? I didn't"
"What?" I was confused.
"That note, it means something to you"
"Of course it does"
"Because you mean everything it says"
"Yes"
I could see the upset in her beautiful eyes.
"If you love me, why would you do this?" she asked, crying "You love me. Why would you leave me? Why would you leave me behind? Alone. Why would you leave me alone?"
This was unexpected. I knew she'd be upset, I had imagined the whole scene in my head: Her, curled up on the floor, crying, clutching the note. But she would get over it, and live out her life. Then I remembered what I had suspected all along; she was scared of being alone. She hadn't wanted to go back to the flat the other night, because it was empty. She didn't want to be there all alone. She shared a flat because she *needed* to. Not because of the money; she needed people around her. The constant parties, going out for lunch, going to the gym. She didn't have to go to the gym every day, she was naturally slim. She *needed* to. To be around people.
"Oh my God Abi" I said "I'm so sorry"
"You were going to leave me behind" she sobbed. Her resolve had gone now. The strength gone. She had crashed.
I took her in my arms "I'm so sorry"

"I don't want to be without you" she said.
"I'm sorry. I'm so sorry" I felt like dirt. She was right; I was going to kill myself to spite mum. To make her feel bad. To make her see what she had done to me.
It hadn't been about Sean at all. My mind had tricked me into thinking it was, but it wasn't. She was right. This beautiful woman, who loved me, was right.
I was going to leave her behind.
And my dad. And James. What the hell was wrong with me?
She stood suddenly, and started pacing around the garden, composing herself.
When she had done so, she sat back down.
"Look Kate, you remember when I told you on the bridge that you were wrong? About me not knowing what it's like. I did it. I tried it. But I couldn't. After I told my parents I was gay, and they had basically disowned me, I tried it. I got in the bath, and slid under the water. I was ready. I had nobody left to upset after all. You know what stopped me?"
"No"
"Not a profound realisation or some sort of heavenly vision. It was the cat. The bloody cat. It jumped into the water. I shit myself, and got out. The bloody cat stopped me. I was angry. Very angry. I could have kicked it. But I didn't. You know why?"
"No"
"Because it made me think. Why the hell was I doing it? Why was I so ready to kill myself? You know why Kate?"
"To spite your parents"
"Yes. To spite my bloody parents" she said angrily.

"To make them feel bad. To make them love me again. That's when I decided to cut them out of my life. I was not going to die for them; I was going to live, and bloody well do something with my life. Something for me"

I stared at her, desperately wanting to hold her, hug her, but I didn't.

"You want me to do the same" I said.

"I don't want you to cut out your parents. But I want you to do something for me"

"What?"

"I want you to do something with your life. Not for you, but for *us*. I want you to live for *us*, Kate. That's what I want. I know you're not gay, it was obvious the first time I met you. And, you may have doubts about that in your own mind, but deep down you know I'm right. You're not gay Kate. I am. And you know what? I don't care. I don't care if we never make love again. Because we did. We did it, and it was the best thing I ever did in my life. It will hurt, but I can live without it. As long as I'm with you"

"What are you saying?" I asked.

"I want to be with you Kate. And I think you want to be with me too. It doesn't bother me that you're not gay. You're not even straight. You're just… Kate. I want to live here, with you. I want to go to bed every night, with you. I want to spend every day of my life, with you. I don't care if we never make love again, I just want to be with you. You're right, you know? You're completely right about me. I don't want to be alone"

She paused to wipe tears from her eyes, then continued.

"I'm *terrified* of being alone. All because my parents kicked me out. We're good together Kate. I feel good around you, safe. Tell me you don't feel the same? Tell me you don't, and I'll happily walk out of here and never come back"
Silence.
"Don't leave me" I said.
"Tell me you feel the same"
I looked up "I feel the same. I have felt the same for a long time, since the first time we met. I feel safe with you, my mind leaves me alone when I'm with you. I love you Abi. I love you. And, you're right, I'm not gay. I'm not straight either. I'm just me. But I love you. I want to spend my life with you, I want to sleep with you every night. I want you to live here, I never want you to leave. And I'm so, so sorry for doing this to you"
She didn't respond. Say something! I shouted in my head.
But she didn't. I panicked.
"You need time to think it over. I understand. It's a lot to deal with, and I messed up, and I'm so sorry, I didn't..."
Shut up Kate" she said.
"What?"
"Just shut up"
She stood, and held out her hand. I took it, and she pulled me to my feet.
"I'm so sorry Abi" I said, crying. I didn't think I had any tears left. But I was wrong.
"You mean all of that?" She asked.
"What? Of course I do? Why..."
I didn't get to finish.

She pulled me into her arms and kissed me. Deeply.
I never wanted to be parted from this woman ever again.
She let go and said "That's how normal women feel Kate. You *are* a normal woman. You see?"
She was right.
I was a normal woman. Because she made me one. She made me normal. *She* did.
It was her; it always had been, and always would be.

-The End -

30. Outro.

I'm not going to lie; I had tears in my eyes when I wrote chapter 27. It was something else.
It was written after I'd almost finished Chapter 25. I was listening to Ryuichi Sakamoto's Merry Christmas Mr Lawrence as I wrote. It really is a beautiful piece of music. You should give it a listen. Listen to the version from the album *Playing the Piano*.

I hope you enjoyed Kate H.
It was an absolute joy to write, if not a little strange. Writing from a woman's perspective as a man is not always easy. I hope I did ok. I wrote this book in the 8 days between 30 Jun and 08 July. It just flowed out. A rarity.

I am currently busy writing the same story from Abigail's perspective. It's whole different read, and incredibly difficult to write. It'll probably be published in early August.

Thank you for reading,

Mike.
Plymstock, July 2025.

31. Alternate Ending.

I wanted to tell you something; the ending of this book was originally different. I've added in the original ending, so you can decide which one was best.

1. Merry Christmas, Mr Lawrence.

I woke up to the sounds of birdsong through my open window. The sun filtered in through gaps in the curtains, giving an enticing glimpse of the beauty waiting beyond. The bed next to me was empty, and the mattress long cold. She had left very early.
I checked my phone; 07.05, Friday, 21 August. The weather was going to be nice all day.
I stretched, and got out of bed. The cat, which had been sleeping at the foot of the bed, jumped down and meowed sweetly. She wanted food.
"Come on Tab" I smiled.
She followed me out, and I overfilled her bowl.
"You're a lovely cat" I said, stroking her "Be good"
I had a tidy round, making sure everything was perfect, then had a shower. After, I dried and dressed my hair, applied my makeup, and chose my best underwear.
I took my time getting ready; I wanted to look my best today. I smiled at my reflection as I checked myself before heading out. It wasn't going to get any better than this. Perfect.
I left my lovely home behind, and walked into the town. There weren't many people around, as the tourist season was almost over now. Traffic was busy, as it always was during rush hour, but it didn't bother me today.
I walked to Marco's to get my usual coffee.
Above me, cirrus clouds feathered the sky.
It reminded me of Abi. Sweet Abi, keeper of my heart.

"Ah, bella signora Kate" Marco smiled as I walked in.
"Morning Marco"
"You look beautiful today, you have important meeting?"
"You could say that" I smiled.
"Ah, I knew. You sit, I make you coffee"
"You're a sweet man Marco"
He brought my coffee a few minutes later, together with the usual cannoli.
"You knock them dead" he smiled "Is that what they say?"
"Yes it is" I smiled. I kissed his cheek "Thank you Marco"
"You have good day signora Kate"
"You too Marco, and thank you"

I walked along the river, sipping my coffee. It really was a beautiful day, I was very grateful for that at least. The geese swam over as soon as I came near the water's edge.
"Sorry geese, I have nothing" I smiled.
Unperturbed, they followed me as I walked along, until I finally lost sight of them behind a bush. I walked on towards the church. I wanted to see Mary today, it had been such a long time since I had last visited. I picked some late blooming flowers to make up for it.
The sun beams filtered through the trees, throwing spotlights on some of the headstones. But not Mary's. How very typical, I thought.
"Morning Mary" I said, stroking her headstone.
I knelt down and placed the flowers on her grave.

"I'm sorry Mary. It's been such a long time, and I really wish I could sit and chat. But, I have an appointment. I'll see you soon though"

I walked out of the graveyard and headed towards the river. I could hear the water rushing over the weir as I approached. A lone Heron sat at the bottom of the rushing water, waiting patiently for a fish to fly past. It really was a beautiful day.

Just up ahead, I heard the rushing traffic on the main road. It was busy and noisy.

The noise increased in volume as I got nearer, and I put my earphones in to deaden the sound. The beautiful tones of Ryuichi Sakamoto's Merry Christmas Mr Lawrence filled my senses. Its beauty calming my nerves. That's better, I thought. I can concentrate now. I walked up to the bridge that crossed the river.

The path on the other side headed back towards the town and the life I knew.

However, I wasn't going that way today. I placed my coffee and cannoli on the handrail. Cars rushed past in a muted form of madness. Up ahead, I saw it coming.

I moved forward and closed my eyes in readiness.

"Oh Sean" I said, and stepped off the edge into the space beyond.

2. The Lights Die Down.

Kathrina Harrington was no more. She hadn't meant it to end this way; she was supposed to have had a long, happy life with her love, Abigail. But, the mind is a powerful master, able to break even the strongest spirit. Given enough time... And it'd had more than enough time to break Kathrina Harrington to the point where she couldn't see the sense in going on anymore. The only way forward was to stop.

Back in the bungalow, she had left notes for her friends: Abi and Mark. There were also separate notes for her mother, father, and brother.
The cat had ample food to last the day.
Abi would come at around five, she'd be worried as Kate wouldn't have answered any of her messages throughout the day. She would take care of her Tabby Tabitha.

Abi walked up the drive with an uneasy feeling in her stomach. She knocked, but there was no response. She tried the door; it was unlocked.
She entered a spotless, empty house. She looked around but found nobody home. On the calendar pinned to the kitchen wall, she noticed something written in bold red letters under today's date: *SEAN*.
She looked around. The only things out of place were five named envelopes laid out carefully on the kitchen table. Next to them; her phone.

Oh no…

With shaking hands, she picked up the envelope bearing her name and opened it. It smelled of Coco Chanel.

Tears were already streaming down her face as she unfolded the note.

My beautiful Abigail,

I want to thank you for making my life so beautifully wonderful over the last few months. You were the first person I think I ever loved, and the only person I ever made love to. For that, I thank you.
I told you when I first met you that I could feel alone, even when I was with you. And I recall the conversation we had about what I should do if I ever feared the worst. I'm so sorry my love, I failed.
If there is anything that should bring you comfort, it is that I am at peace now. No more pain. No more negativity. No more masks. I'm finally free.
Don't think badly of me my love, I can do that for both of us. Instead, remember me fondly, and with love.

Look around you, this home I created is yours now.
In fact, everything I own is now yours, officially.
My lasting gift to you. I won't blame you if you sell the house, so don't worry; it's what a normal woman would do.

Think of me when you see cirrus clouds above.
I love you, and only you.

Kathrina. X.

She fell to her knees. She vaguely remembered seeing a local news item on her phone during her lunchbreak, about a young woman who had jumped in front of a speeding truck during rush hour that morning. She had scrolled past it, giving it little thought.

She clutched the note to her chest and fell onto her side, curling up on the floor, sobbing uncontrollably.

The light had just gone out of her life.

Her beautiful Kate was gone.

- The End -

Printed in Dunstable, United Kingdom